D1169623

THE·FIRST·FALL

THE · FIRST · FALL

YTTERBOE HALL · AUTUMN 1946

A novel by Steve Swanson

Nine Ten Press
Northfield, Minnesota
55057-0505

First Printing, May, 1997

Copyright © 1997 by Steve Swanson
Library of Congress Catalog Card Number: 97-91691

ISBN   0-9657762-0-4

Cover and interior design by Judy Swanson

Editor, Shelley Swanson Sateren

Printed in the United States of America

Dedicated to the founders of St. Olaf College, especially Halvor T. Ytterboe, martyr, to many generations of their faithful successors, and to thousands of denizens of Ytterboe Hall, 1900-1997.

ACKNOWLEDGMENTS

Thanks to those who read earlier versions of this story, and who encouraged and enabled its publication:

Ron Klug, Stan Frear, Carol Lysne, Scott
Swanson, Karen Hansen, Beth Gettys Sturkey,
Mark Allister, Gerry Thorson, Lowell Johnson,
Kris Paulson, Dan Jorgenson, Judy Swanson,
Shelley Swanson Sateren, and Alan Marks and
his staff—especially Linda.

The publication of this novel was timed to help St. Olaf College alumni, staff, and students commemorate the decommissioning of Ytterboe Hall on May 24, 1997.

•

If you are not my late father—or a mid-century Northfielder mentioned by name herein—and think you recognize yourself, or me, or someone else in this fiction, you have more imagination than I do.

Steve Swanson

PREFACE

In 1946, after several low enrollment war years, St. Olaf College admitted 261 freshman women and 488 freshman men. Of the previous spring's 125 graduating seniors, only eleven were men. Almost overnight, St. Olaf's enrollment had increased by one-third, and for the first time ever, freshmen numbered almost half of the total student body. The men were back.

Ytterboe (IT-er-boe) Hall housed more than two thirds of those freshman men—many of them older veterans on the GI Bill.

The First Fall is a story about students who might have attended St. Olaf in that era. Although the characters are fictional, the places are real. Ytterboe Hall, a red brick men's dormitory, the largest building in Northfield, Minnesota, for nearly a half century, stood on campus from 1900 to 1997.

First called Boys' Hall, the building was renamed Ytterboe Hall in 1914, a decade after Professor Halvor T. Ytterboe died at age 46 of formaldehyde poisoning. He had fumigated the hall's only toilet daily for ten weeks, trying to control a scarlatina epidemic among the dormitory's residents. The exposure proved to be lethal.

As his illness progressed, a sickroom was prepared for Professor Ytterboe on the third floor of the dormitory. From that window, he could watch comings and goings at the front door. He was borne out of that door to a horse-drawn hearse on February 26, 1904.

Professor Ytterboe was resident head of the dorm in its first years. St. Olaf historian Joe Shaw describes Ytterboe as a tall, deep-voiced, imposing man with a red pompadour and mustache, stern but popular, and crazy about baseball. Starting in 1882, he taught Latin, Norwegian, English, geography, didactics, and hygiene six hours a day, six days a week. After Boys' Hall was built, he rode herd on all of the college's young men twenty-four hours a day, seven days a week. He also acted as the school's business manager and registrar. Professor Ytterboe literally saved the college with his inspired and untiring fund-raising efforts during the depression of 1893-1899.

Almost all twentieth century St. Olaf College men lived in Ytterboe Hall. With the coming of co-ed dorms in the seventies, some corridors in the building also housed women. The building's history is overladen with legend, lore, myth, and memories.

Only a few of those memories are wrapped into this story. If you want more, just ask Joe Shaw, or any other St. Olaf graduate over age twenty-five.

Steve Swanson, class of '54

I am interested in human beings . . . Human portraiture has no end. It is as manifold and inexhaustible as life itself.

From the foreword
The Boat of Longing
Ole Edvart Rolvaag
1921

1

She was crying.

"Jon?" she managed to say.

"I've heard," he said harshly, the phone mashing his ear. They were using their forty years in the developing non sequitur short-speak. "They announced it in chapel. I went over to the student center and bought a newspaper." He ran his fingers over the obituary folded open on his desk.

"I'm sorry," she said and sniffed. "It's been one of those days." After a long pause punctuated with several more sniffles, she added, "The Development Office called. Something about an endowment Tony set up."

"Why would that have anything to do with me?"

"I don't know. I don't know anything. Why do we always have to argue every time his name comes up?"

"He's dead. So the arguing ends," he said.

"You should have forgiven him years ago. And if you didn't back then, you should now."

"You can only forgive the living."

"Well, then *forget*."

They hung up in silence, an unusual end to one of their conversations. Usually one of them would say, "Goodbye. I love you," and the other would respond, "Not as much as I love you," to which the other would counter, "That's what you think," dripping with exchanged affection.

Dr. Jonathan Adamson, 68, professor of History, St. Olaf College, Northfield, Minnesota, slipped the phone back into its cradle and leaned back in his office chair. He swung the chair around and stared out his office window toward Rolvaag Memorial Library.

Adamson laced his fingers behind his head and inhaled stale air. Moments later the air escaped in a deep sigh. He knew he'd have to make some kind of peace with Tony's death.

But not yet.

Old memories that had haunted him often for fifty years became more pronounced since the history department had assigned him an office in Ytterboe Hall eight years earlier. He had avoided the building until that office assignment had forced him to face his ghosts.

But he hadn't faced them yet, not really. In eight years he hadn't once gone up to second floor, having created imaginative excuses to avoid it. "Why don't we meet at the Cage?" "Why don't you come down to my office instead?" he would suggest to colleagues who had offices on the second floor.

And yet memories drifted down to his first floor office from the attic and from the second floor like a gas heavier than air—like carbon dioxide in a silo—invisible but threatening.

Adamson stared at the obituary again. He saw "REGENT" in the headline. He knew that Tony had honestly loved St. Olaf College. As a regent he'd ridden herd on two years of downsizing, tried to make it as painless as possible for St. Olaf, using techniques he'd learned at 3M. "A church college shouldn't crucify its employees," he was quoted as saying.

Just before he died, Tony had been on campus for a tiring battery of meetings, and for a gala Syttende Mai chapel service and celebration.

Fifty years earlier Jonathan Adamson and Anthony Tarpezi had started out as roommates, classmates, almost friends—and had ended as enemies.

Adamson glanced over at his filing cabinet. The whole long story was filed in there, scribbled in his old journals.

He moved his rolling office chair back a couple of feet from his desk and pulled his knees up. He pushed against the desk and rotated slowly in a full circle, surveying his books, journals, posters, prints, framed certificates, a page of Holinshed, a bust of Tacitus.

Over the years, he had been assigned offices in five buildings on the St. Olaf campus. This, he knew, would be his last. *Neither Ytterboe Hall nor this old history professor is long for this college,* he admitted to himself. *The building will be torn down this summer and I'm retiring. Done in one week.*

A wave of emotion washed over him. He leaned back and studied the cracked and bulging walls of his office, reminding himself that nearly two hundred St. Olaf College students had lived in this room during the ninety years the building had been a dormitory.

In the early days they were *new* walls, lath and plaster—plumb, uncracked, and patchless, walls that framed smooth ceilings above and level floors below. Now the place looked more like an urban crack house. In the winter the sprinkler system always froze and cracked. The roof leaked. Prudent faculty members draped plastic sheets over their books and computers every night, summer and winter.

Adamson knew from hearsay that thrill-bound students haunted the upper floors at night, gaining entry by boosting and pulling each other up on the exterior iron fire escapes, then forcing windows open. Some of them boasted of seeing midnight ghosts.

Adamson's own ghosts dated back to fall semester, 1946.

He spun his chair back toward the desk, doing a quick check of its framed pictures, reminding himself that—so far so good—he was alive and well and so were his wife, kids, and grandkids. *Doing okay. Better than this building,* he thought. July 2, 1997, eight o'clock in the morning, the machines would tear into it.

I'm glad it's going down, he acknowledged to himself. Bury my ghosts. Purge my demons.

Adamson knew that third generation descendants of Professor Ytterboe and some nostalgic and vocal alumni had objected to razing the building. But why honor, he asked himself, a venerable and martyred founder like Halvor Ytterboe with the vulnerable and crumbling mortar of such a floundering old building?

Back in 1900 they had skimped on the foundation. Neglecting foundations was a problem Adamson often mused upon—in buildings, in institutions—and in people.

For a moment Adamson tried to envision the demolition of old Ytterboe. They'll need a crane first, he thought, to take the cupola off the top. They'd have to save that at least. Maybe make some sort of campus monument out of it.

He thought about the domed cupola, smiling at the Harvard-of-the-Westers who had begun to call it a belvedere. He glanced again at the obituary lying on his desk. Suddenly the memory of a hot September night up in the cupola fifty years earlier flashed through his mind. He slowly traced his finger over the obituary's newsprint headline:

ANTHONY TARPEZI, WAS 3M EXECUTIVE AND ST. OLAF COLLEGE REGENT

Tears came to Adamson's eyes.

"Damn you, Tony the Torpedo," he whispered. "Damn you."

Adamson swallowed back the curse as he spoke the words. No matter what Tony had done, he didn't deserve hell. Tony believed in purgatory. Let him enjoy it, thought Adamson.

Adamson wiped his eyes and pulled his mind away from past incriminations and sour memories to present-tense wrecking balls and huge backhoes and dump trucks that would cart this condemned building away to a demolition landfill, load by scrambled load.

Adamson glanced at the administrative memo taped to the

wall above his desk:

> Following the decommissioning ceremonies on May 24, Ytterboe Hall must be emptied. All offices must be cleared of personal effects by June 1 so that maintenance personnel can remove office furnishings. Demolition begins July 2.

Start sorting, he told himself. Syttende Mai, May 17, was last Saturday. Norwegian Independence Day. Why, he asked himself, don't I feel more independent, more free? I'm retiring. This is my last week. One week to sort out junk. Save some, recycle some, dump the rest. One week and I'm gone. One month from now this place will look like a war zone.

Adamson fought off the temptation to think about Tony and the war. He rolled his chair over to the filing cabinet and stood up. He slid open the top metal drawer a couple of inches. The century-old floor sagged away from the wall so steeply that the drawer rolled out the rest of the way unassisted.

He ran his fingers over the manila file folders the way his grandma's friends used to fondle her Sarah Hadley Battenberg lace.

The very antithesis of a computer's speed-demon hard disk, his manila files contained slow memories of former students, former times—paper copy—some of it as precious to him as the Khumran scrolls. He hated with a deep passion the blind speed, do-it-now immediacy that computers and e-mail and voice mail had brought to his life. Deep inside he knew himself to have an anti-technology, neo-Luddite mentality.

Most of these folders had to be dumped. Today. He knew he should have started weeks earlier.

Adamson dragged an office paper recycling bin in from the hall. He began to pull folders of student writing and dump them by the fistful into the bin.

RESEARCH PAPERS, KEEPERS. HONORS PAPERS, 1975.

HONORS PAPERS, 1976. PARACOLLEGE PROJECTS. He dumped them all. He pushed the now nearly empty drawer closed, marveling that its rollers had carried so easily the fifty paper pounds and a thirty year record of his classroom history. He stared at the drawer, suddenly seeing instead a cold storage locker in a morgue.

She'll want to go to his funeral, he thought. Do I go with her? Can I make myself?

Adamson yanked open another drawer and started humming a Sunday School song about death that he'd learned almost sixty years earlier in Grandma Brindley's Episcopal church. He always struggled to remember the words, unsure especially of the fourth line which he could never recollect exactly:

> The bells of hell go ding-a-ling-a-ling
> For you but not for me
> For me the angels sing-a-ling-a-ling
> They've got the goods for me
> O death where is thy sting-a-ling-a-ling
> O grave thy victory
> The bells of hell go ding-a-ling-a-ling
> For you but not for me.

Cruel song to teach kids, he thought. You're going to hell and I'm not.

Adamson began to toss more files, this time his own writing. HISTORY 375 LECTURES. OPENING CONVOCATION ADDRESS FOR 1985. INTRO TEXTBOOK—a freshman text that he and Joe Shaw had outlined together but had never written.

Most important to him in the middle drawer were his journals. He would *not* toss those.

Back in high school he had begun to write something like a diary—not every day, but, like a budding dramatist, sketchy acts and scenes and lines that seemed worth recording. He'd filed them episodically. HIGH SCHOOL. COLLEGE, FRESHMAN

YEAR. GRADUATE SCHOOL.

Behind them all, way in back, was a manila envelope marked RR. A stranger might incorrectly guess the acronym stood for Rolls Royce in spite of Adamson's twenty-year love affair with Volvo 240's.

Adamson alone knew the meaning of RR and what the folder contained. It was a secret he'd kept even from his wife.

Certainly she won't let me move all these files home, he thought. Certainly not that one. He snapped it with a fingernail. He knew the college archivist wouldn't want many of his scribblings either—except for a few from the early days—like the notes he'd saved from the now world-famous composer, F. Melius Christiansen, when, as a boy, he used to mow F. Melius's lawn.

Adamson pulled the FRESHMAN YEAR folder out of the drawer. He mused on the title for a moment. We can't even call it fresh*man* any more, he thought with a snort. Now it has to be the more politically correct "First Year." Postmen are women, God is my mother, and all freshmen are neuter, he muttered. Fresh persons. Stale persons. Where will it end? He shook his head and started to open the folder.

A sudden knock at the door made him slam the folder shut and drop it upside down on his desk top.

"Dr. Adamson?"

He automatically checked his fly, checked his eyes for tears with the knuckle of an index finger, then called, "Come in."

The door opened tentatively. The long thin face of a young woman peered in. When she saw he was alone, she swung the door wide and stood there with an uncomfortable and false confidence, feet apart, her "self" framed in the open doorway.

Her large black eyes seemed gigantic behind small wire-framed glasses. The whole visage was embraced by even blacker hair that like a dark river forked willingly around the oval island of her face, then cascaded over her shoulders, splaying over her breasts.

Jennifer Jankowski. A junior. As un-Norwegian as Tony had

been. Jenn-Jan, as he'd heard other students call her, was a student in his contemporary history seminar. The name reminded him of Flo-Jo, the Olympic runner. He smiled, thinking of Flo-Jo's slow-mo fluid beauty exploding out of the blocks. He'd seen Flo-Jo in an airport a year earlier, her trademark fingernails, claws four inches long, painted iridescent green.

"Is something funny, Professor Adamson?" Jennifer asked, a smile dancing across her lips.

"I was smiling at your nickname, Jenn-Jan, and thinking of Flo-Jo."

Her smile vanished. She looked puzzled. Jennifer, like most St. Olaf four point oh curve raisers, was driven to know all answers. She wouldn't ask him for an explanation just then, but Adamson knew that she'd look up Flo-Jo in a contemporary biography the next trip to the library reference room.

Could it be that she's never even heard of Flo-Jo? Adamson wondered. Is Flo-Jo already a no-go? A has-been?

He shook off his Olympic musings and opened the French scene like a trained actor, reminding himself that this was not Act I of either *Pygmalion* or *The Education of Rita*. Jennifer Jankowski was neither Rita nor Liza Doolittle. Jenn-Jan was no Cockney street creature that some frustrated professor needed to mold into a goddess. Jennifer Jankowski had come to St. Olaf well trained, bright, and articulate, her language and research habits nearly immaculate from the start. She needed little from him but encouragement.

Considering them scum, and naming a few as he thought about it, Adamson could understand, as he looked at Jennifer, how some professors might have affairs with their students. Profs' favorites were always just like Jennifer—eager, attractive, and vulnerable. They reminded aging profs of their old flames—and that the fire was dying out.

Sometimes, he thought, looking at Jennifer, no one had ever before valued these young women for their minds, or recognized or encouraged or supported their talents. Few of these young women had ever before entrusted an adult authority figure with their ideas. Teachers who betrayed that trust were *worse* than scum, Adamson decided.

Jennifer shifted her feet in a quiet shuffle. Adamson blinked and remembered that he was in a scene. He went back to his supporting actor lines.

"Your essay at last?" he asked her, dropping his tethered glasses to his chest in a bit of professorial stage business.

"Sorry it's late." She picked up the cue. The scene was launched. "This one was hard to write," she added, gesturing with the manuscript she held in her right hand. Tennessee Williams would have called for a gesture more bold and suggestive.

Adamson already had most of her classmates' essays piled on his desk. "History in the Making," he called the course. He always invited guest speakers to come and talk for a class period about the era they had lived through. He'd had dozens of guests over the years—most of them St. Olaf alumni, most of them friends: ex-governors, missionaries, composers, teachers, an Auschwitz survivor, a retired Ringling Brothers clown.

The course was popular, partly because of the guests, but also because it made students think about both the ephemeral and the lasting issues they themselves were living through. Because Jennifer said she'd had difficulty writing her paper, Adamson guessed aloud at her approach.

"You must have chosen the autobiographical option then," he said.

"I did. It was painful."

"Writing about ourselves often is."

"I tried to be honest."

"Good."

A long pause followed. Jennifer didn't offer him the essay or move from the doorway.

"I'm not sure I want you to read it," she finally said. The essay inched its way up to her chest. She held it there, clamped possessively under her crossed arms. If this had been a scene in a movie, the camera would have pulled in for a closeup of the manuscript, her hands, her breasts.

Does she expect me to tear it away from her by main force? wondered Adamson.

"If you really don't want me to read it," he said, shaking off the absurd Monty Python-esque image of an old professor wrestling an essay away from a cowering student, "then take another few days and write a different one."

Adamson watched that idea take root behind her eyes.

"No," she said. "I don't have time. I have to write my finals. This is it. Even if you hate me for it."

"Nothing could make me hate you, Jennifer. Or even dislike you."

"That's what's so neat about you, Doctor Adamson," she said, lowering her eyes. Her genuine compliment appeared to have made her feel awkward.

Something about this Jennifer co-ed had a disturbing effect on Adamson. Suddenly he realized what it was. Her hair. Her silky dark hair. Vague and distant memories suddenly flooded back. Rhonda.

Adamson felt his eyes moist over. He quickly turned to his desk and was confronted with the obituary. Rhonda and Tony. He struggled for composure. It only partly worked.

"Is something wrong, Doctor Adamson?" she asked and took a half step forward. Then she stopped, appearing to have remembered her place as student.

After an embarrassingly long pause, Adamson's voice returned. Tears were filling his eyes. He was coming unstrung before one of his students.

"One of my wife's friends just died," was all he could manage.

Telling her that she looked like a fifty-year-old memory would have raised more questions—and he certainly didn't feel like discussing it with her, or anyone.

"I'm sorry," she said quietly. At last she released the manuscript from her chest like a memorial flower, and offered it to him.

Rhonda, thought Adamson. The hands. The face. Beautiful, enchanting Rhonda. He fought back more tears.

He stretched out his arm to receive her paper but was unable to look up and face Rhonda's modern day look-alike, Jennifer Jankowski.

Of course Jennifer wasn't even remotely aware that she was starring in a romantic drama written fifty years earlier. Finally, in a resigned sort of way which suggested that maybe all professors were weird, she asked, "Is there anything I can do?"

"No. No, thanks," he said, shaking his head, wishing to the depths of his being that there was something her youth and beauty could still give him.

She laid the manuscript on his open palm.

"Are you sure you're all right?" she asked.

"I'm fine."

"Okay, then, if you're sure."

"I'm sure."

Suddenly, probably from growing embarrassment and as if transformed by a magic wand, she became carefree, childlike, and skipped back out the door.

"See ya," she said, clicking the heavy old door shut. There the scene ended.

Trying to shake off the memories tugging at his tear ducts, Adamson deliberately, angrily pushed a few books and papers aside, being careful in his pique not to crumple the folded obituary. He dropped Jennifer's paper into the small space he had cleared on his desk top. He reached for the glasses suspended like a miniature window-washing scaffold against his chest, using both hands to hook them behind his drooping ears. With three fingers of his right hand he pinched the pads onto the bridge of his nose, then stared at the paper for a moment before beginning to read.

The essay was neat, as expected, and coming from Jennifer he would also expect the piece to be well organized and brightly crafted.

MY OWN PERSONAL SEXUAL REVOLUTION
by Jennifer Jankowski

I had sex for the first time when I was thirteen—with
my cousin Jeff. It was not fun...

As usual, hers was a quick and snappy opening paragraph.
Always a grabber. He knew he could give her essay an A without
even reading it. But he very much wanted to read it.

As a young teacher he would have been mortified if a student
had handed in such a confessional essay. It wouldn't have happened. No one back then would have submitted such honest work.

In the last couple of decades he'd learned not to be shocked
by anything. Just a week earlier a student had told him, as casually as if passing on baseball box scores, that his father had had an
affair with their pastor—a woman—because his mother was les-
bian.

Hardly a quirk, or kink, or concupiscence that he might dream
up would be half as strange as what he heard almost daily from
students or colleagues. They dumped it on him too, knowing he'd
listen and not judge. Jennifer Jankowski felt a permission that was
never spoken aloud, but which Adamson cherished in his relationship with students. She and her classmates seemed to be aware
that they could write whatever they wanted, knowing Adamson
would grade their work as history and as writing.

Her essay attracted him, not for prurient reasons, in light of its
title, but because he was always fascinated by the lives of his students and the way their minds worked.

Adamson leaned back in his chair and looked upward. He pictured the dormitory rooms on the second floor, beyond the
cracked plaster of his office ceiling.

"My own sexual revolution," he said aloud, "started nearly fifty
years ago—right here in this building." He mentally scanned the
second floor rooms over his head and allowed his memories to tip-
toe down the hallway to room 223.

12

His mind's eye located the door. He had not dared to return to the second floor or to confront room 223's door for fifty years. Room 223. "Our room," he said and sighed. "I'm sure it's still there."

Like some huge, soon-to-be-extinct creature, Ytterboe Hall had left broad and deep footprints embedded in the clay of his life's riverbed.

Adamson reached down and spread the fingers of his wrinkled right hand wide upon Jennifer's confessional essay. He was in no mood for the interesting and engaging reading it was sure to be. He began nevertheless, peeking between his fingers like a schoolboy, reading her words compulsively.

At the beginning of her second paragraph he stopped suddenly. He pulled Tony's obituary out from underneath Jennifer's manuscript and laid the newsprint over her manicured paragraphs. Tony.

ANTHONY TARPEZI, WAS 3M EXECUTIVE
AND ST. OLAF COLLEGE REGENT

Adamson stared at the obituary and the tears began again. Regret, anguish, alienation, betrayal. A dozen might have beens.

He grabbed his FRESHMAN YEAR folder resolutely and slapped it harshly down on top of Tony's obituary. "Let's just see," he muttered to himself and sniffed loudly.

He glanced out the window at the gathering May evening, then turned back to his desk and stared at the folder. He suddenly, decisively, flipped open the story of his young life. His eyes sank deeply into the fifty-year-old copy.

"Did Tony have to die to make me ready for this?" he asked the quiet room.

He allowed himself then to read and to remember.

2

Jonathan Adamson stood in front of the bakery window and studied first the caramel rolls, then the cherry and blueberry pies, then the Norwegian crown cake—then her.

Disturbed that the glass distorted her image, Jon fixed his eyes upon her nevertheless. He continued to stare until she startled him by turning her head slightly in his direction. Yet it seemed, as always, that he remained invisible to her.

Because she worked there, the Northfield Bakery drew Jon like a magnet draws iron filings. She was his pole star, his Mecca, his magnetic field. As a cover for his daily visits, Jon had spent many of his scarce summer dollars on cookies and doughnuts for himself and bread for his parents. And because she usually ran the soda fountain, he'd also bought enough fountain cokes and malts to rot nearly all his teeth.

She never noticed him. She'd worked there an entire year and Jon had hung around so often, yet he still felt like a phantom. She was pleasant enough, but it seemed she'd never really *seen* him. Among a group of ten strangers, he thought with a sigh, she might not even recognize me as a Northfielder.

Well, *today* I'm going to talk to her, Jon told himself that hot August morning. We start college next week and she'll start meeting upperclassmen. Older guys. I have to snag her attention, her affection, first. It's now or nev— No, thought Jon with determination. I'll never say "never" when it comes to her.

Jon walked boldly into the shop and in his haste let the screen door bang loudly behind him. Everyone turned and looked.

"Oops. Sorry," he blurted, then took his place in line behind a woman he knew, Mrs. Tufte.

"A dozen glazed doughnuts," Mrs. Tufte said to the goddess behind the counter.

"Right," said the goddess. She swung open the glass showcase door and, using tongs, lifted twelve golden orbs into a white paper sack. The scene was celestial.

Jon studied the firm squareness of her shoulders, her long eyelashes, the fawn hue and softness of her cheek, her slim waist and the smooth roundness of her hips. He adored her beautiful hands.

"Anything else?" the angel asked.

"No, that's all today."

Before Mrs. Tufte could turn away, the angel asked, "Are you going back to the bank?"

"Yes, I am."

"Could I send a note for Mr. Peterson?"

"Of course."

The queen pulled a green and white newsprint counter receipt pad from the pocket of her red apron, peeled off a sheet and turned it over. She pulled out the golden pencil she always had tucked through her black hair in the channel above her delicate right ear.

The queen wrote carefully and intently for a minute, signed her name, but then, just before she handed it over, crumpled the note into a ball in the palm of her hand.

"On second thought," she said, "I'll stop by the bank at one o'clock, right after lunch. Thanks anyway."

The siren set the ball of paper on the counter, said thank you to Mrs. Tufte, then looked at Jon—not at his eyes exactly, but at the center of his forehead. The word "pimple" popped into his mind and he felt a wave of anguish.

"What can I do for you?" the siren asked him.

You can fall in love with me, Jon wanted to say. You can go out with me every weekend all next year, he longed to say.

He knew he couldn't bring himself to utter such words, but he had rehearsed carefully an introduction. Hi, I'm Jon Adamson, he planned to say boldly, and since we'll both be freshmen at St. Olaf this year, I thought we should get to know each other. Really well.

But when the princess looked at him with her brown eyes, all he could think of was almonds. "D-do you have anything with. . .almonds?"

"Cookies," she said.

"A half dozen," he said.

She turned away to bag up the cookies. Jon grabbed the crumpled ball of receipt pad paper and slipped it into his jeans pocket.

"Thirty-five cents," she said, turning back to the counter with the small white bag.

Jon nervously pulled a handful of coins out of his pocket and dropped a quarter on the floor. It rolled under the bench of an empty booth. He fell to his knees and scrambled after the runaway quarter. When he jumped back to his feet, she was smiling.

"Sorry," he said, blushing. He laid the quarter and a dime on the glass counter top, wishing she'd reached out so he could've placed his worship offering in her hand, perhaps touching her delicate skin.

"It's okay," she said, then turned away to greet the next a-mused customer.

Jon walked out of the store staring at the bag of cookies. I don't even like almond cookies, he thought with a deep sigh.

But then he smiled, remembering suddenly the crumpled note stuffed in his jeans.

Jon hurried the half block to Bridge Square, dropped the bag of cookies beside him on a green slat park bench, then dug her note out of his pocket. He sat down and smoothed it carefully with both hands over the roundness of his thigh. It read:

Mr. Peterson—

I'll be in this afternoon to check on my
college loan. Thanks,

Rhonda Rasmussen

There it was. Her whole beautiful poetic name in her own
lovely handwriting: Rhonda Rasmussen.

Jon folded the note once and put it in the cookie bag. He
picked up his bike that he'd left in the grass and clipped the bag
under the snaps on his bookrack. He rode over the bridge, up
over the tracks, and pedaled up the hill toward 918 West Second
Street.

At home in his room, Jon pulled a shoe box from his desk
drawer, retrieved the note from the cookie bag, and smoothed it
carefully. He laid the note on top of a favorite Rhonda treasure,
her picture clipped from the *Northfield News,* her glamorous features vivid in stage makeup, her hair braided in double pigtails for
the role of Dorothy in a community theater program of songs from
The Wizard of Oz the previous summer.

Along with the clipping, Jon kept an even more treasured
memento—an autographed program from the show. "Next stop,
Hollywood," she'd penned on the program, then signed it "Rhonda."
He had stood in line for ten minutes to get her autograph. She
hadn't noticed him then either.

The box held several other priceless Rhonda artifacts—a stick
of Juicy Fruit gum, well chewed and rolled in its wrapper, a hair
comb with a single long black hair in it, and a well-worn movie theater ticket stub—things she had chewed, touched, used—and he
had collected, precious few treasures for so many hours of shad-
owy stealth.

She had flicked the gum into the grass one afternoon as she
stood looking at the river across from the post office. Jon searched
a quarter of an hour on his hands and knees to find it. The comb
she had left behind in a booth at Cronholm's Riverside Cafe.

She dropped the ticket stub on her way in to see *Spellbound*. Jon sat two rows behind her and during the entire Hitchcock film rubbed the ticket stub between his thumb and forefinger as he studied Rhonda. He hardly noticed Ingrid Bergman. He was distracted from Rhonda only momentarily when, at the end of the film, the gun turned and fired directly at the audience.

After stashing his treasures, Jon plopped on his bed and lay there thinking of her. He knew his feelings for her were madness—but he had never felt that way about anyone before. He had sleuthed and spied and asked questions of anyone and everyone to learn that she lived with her grandparents in Edina. No one knew anything about her parents.

Jon had found her senior picture in a 1945 yearbook in the Edina Public Library. He studied the yearbook and discovered she'd been a cheerleader. She sang in choir and acted in plays. She was an honor student. Jon had been tempted to slit her picture out of the yearbook with his penknife, but the place was teeming with nosy librarians and their scurrying assistants.

Jon had asked questions around Northfield and learned that Rhonda was working during the year after her high school graduation to earn money for college. Her sister and brother-in-law owned the bakery on Northfield's main street.

She also sang in the St. John's Church senior choir, and acted in every community theater production throughout the year. Hundreds of Rhonda sightings were Jon's reward for his ace detective work.

The previous spring at Easter, Rhonda had gone home to Edina and Jon had driven all the way there and managed to find her grandparents' house. He hoped to catch sight of her.

He sat in his car across the street for hours without success. I'm just a kid to her, he told himself as he drove back home, deflated. A high school kid.

And now here it is, August, he thought. College starts next week and Rhonda Rasmussen will still see only a high school kid in me—if she sees me at all.

He tried to imagine every possible shortcut to looking older, to appearing more mature. He grabbed a pulp magazine off his nightstand and scoured the little ads in the back pages. Most of them promised a more beautiful body or instant romance if you only bought their product. But he didn't need to lose weight. He was already skinny. His half-inch hair was too short to change. Elevator shoes were too expensive. A Charles Atlas "98 Pound Weakling" muscle-building course would take too long.

I know, he thought, I'll wear my dad's St. Olaf letterman's jacket next trip to the bakery. But then he remembered the frightening confrontation in the ninth grade. He'd worn his Uncle Lars's Navy Air Force sweater to school one day. Three burly football players, all seniors, stopped him in the hall, pointed to the golden winged N on his chest and said, "You haven't earned a letter in Northfield."

Jon never wore the sweater again.

It was high noon now and the August heat was transforming Jon's room into a sauna. He wiped the sweat from his forehead and dismissed the jacket idea. Too hot, he thought. She'd think I was crazy.

Jon glanced at his alarm clock and suddenly leaped off his bed. Rhonda had said she'd be at the bank at one o'clock. Another chance to see her, maybe talk to her. Jon grabbed his car keys. No time to ride his bike. He sped downtown in his little Model A roadster.

Jon hung around at the mill gas station across from the State Bank for nearly a half hour until Rhonda appeared. He ran across the street and followed her into the bank. He waved nervously to Mrs. Tufte behind the counter, then slipped over to the chest-high marble check writing desk in the center of the lobby. He eavesdropped from there.

Rhonda sat down in front of Mr. Peterson's desk and talked briefly to him. Jon couldn't hear what they said. Then she left. She hadn't noticed Jon.

Jon studied the stained glass dome high above the lobby in the round building, pretending nonchalance. Then he moved to the other side of the marble table so he could watch Rhonda through the front window. She walked across the bridge toward the square, then disappeared from sight.

Jon sighed, his shoulders drooping. He picked up a pad of State Bank of Northfield counter checks from the table, and slapped it nervously several times on the marble table top. He wondered what to try next.

Suddenly Jon grabbed the tethered fountain pen and began to scribble on a counter check. Pay to the order of: RHONDA RASMUSSEN, he printed boldly on the top check. Then he carefully penned, $1,000,000/ONE MILLION DOLLARS. He dated the check August 24, 1946, then signed his name at the bottom.

This would impress her, he thought. She wouldn't need a college loan then. She'd be grateful to me forever.

Yeah, he added, folding the check once and tucking it in his billfold, she'd *have to notice* when the police caught up with him at the bakery and dragged him off to jail for check fraud.

3

Jon slung the newspaper bag over his shoulder and marched out
the front door of his parents' house. He wondered if he looked
like a kid running away from home. He turned right and spotted
Old Main on the hill on the eastern edge of the campus, two
blocks and one grassy slope away.

St. Olaf College had evolved out of a farm town. If it weren't
for Carleton and St. Olaf colleges on its eastern and western hills,
Northfield would have been just another rural river town of houses, grocery stores, hardware stores, car and farm implement deal-
erships—like any other southern Minnesota town with a popula-
tion of four thousand.

Everyone called St. Olaf's campus "The Hill." Its historic
name was "Manitou Heights." Centuries earlier, Indians had given
their sacred campgrounds overlooking the Cannon River this
name.

St. Olaf College stood on Northfield's tallest hill. Many times
during his childhood, Jon had climbed Old Main tower where he
could see many miles in all directions. From that tower he could
actually look *down* on the Carleton College campus across town.

Carleton students took St. Olaf's high altitude in stride. "Built
on a bluff," they chanted at football games, "and run on the same
principle."

This warm Labor Day morning, Jon began his college career

by climbing to the plateau of the campus. He walked west past Old Main, the Steensland Library, the Art Barn, and Holland Hall, then turned northwest and headed for Ytterboe.

Jon stopped deliberately in front of Ytterboe Hall and studied the building for a few moments. Ytterboe's lime rock datestone was embedded high on the front wall, above the heavy double oak doors. It was centered above the hip roof entryway that sheltered the doors and just below the third floor windows. The rectangular datestone was deeply engraved: MCM.

Jon's father told him that years before, early in the century, St. Olaf students often pointed to the MCM and chanted "Many Christian Men" or "Mostly Charter Members." Jon stared at the Roman numerals, pondering a current MCM saying. Jon was starting college in 1946. He'd graduate in 1950. How about "Mid-Century Men?" he thought. Not scintillating, but true.

As a Roman numeral, MCM was easy to decipher—1900. The building would always be the same age as the year. This year, thought Jon, both the century and Ytterboe Hall are forty-six years old. The building already showed its age.

For more than forty years, Ytterboe had been St. Olaf College's only men's dorm. It had ushered in the new century and had seen St. Olaf men through a worldwide depression and two world wars. Thorson Hall, a new men's dorm, was already under construction out on ski-jump hill, and would possibly be ready in time for Jon's junior or senior year.

Jon's eyes scaled Ytterboe's front wall, darted over the eaves, then rested on the slope of the steep gabled roof. Perched atop and in the center of its roof was a white, freshly painted cupola, the size of a small garage, its roof as square as a graduating senior's mortarboard. Centered above its roof was a tin, helmetlike dome. Out of the tip of that dome, like a mast, rose a twenty-five-foot flagpole, blue spruce, Jon guessed, like the mast of a Viking ship. The cupola looked like a quaint Victorian gazebo straddling the steep roof of Ytterboe Hall.

Ytterboe Hall was normally home to 250 St. Olaf men. But

this year Jon knew that the returning GIs had swelled the number to 350. Freshmen were going to be jammed in and Jon had heard rumors that many weren't happy about it. He wondered whether the room he and Anthony Tarpezi were assigned to was originally a single room.

Jon stared at the front door, sighed a big sigh, and thought, Ytterboe is my second home now—or, my home for a second time. He'd lived with his parents in the main floor resident head's quarters during his eighth and ninth grade years.

Jon slung his *Minneapolis Star* newspaper bag over his shoulder and headed up the stairs. The bag seemed heavier than when he had carried papers, heavier even than those Sundays right before the war when there was so much world news and no shortage yet of newsprint paper. There were still plenty of goods and services to advertise for sale. A serviceman back in 1939 was not a soldier dressed in olive green, but someone who fixed your washing machine.

As if to mock the missing load of slim newspapers rich with exciting war zone communiques that he had carried through the early forties, the bag now contained a dull assembly of mundane items that would outfit his dorm room: his portable typewriter, a dictionary, spiral and three-ring notebooks, a small radio, toiletries, and underwear. His mother had for years perversely sewn name tapes into all his clothes—even his underwear and tee shirts. Bedding, he had read in the college mailings, was provided—otherwise Jon's mother would certainly have labeled his sheets as well.

On the first floor landing, Jon stopped and pulled from his billfold—for the tenth time that morning—his room assignment card. He ran his left hand like a winnowing fork through his heinie haircut and read the room number and names:

YTTERBOE HALL 223
Jonathan Adamson, '50
Northfield, Minn.

and
Anthony Tarpezi, '50
Milwaukee, Wis.

They were both freshmen, but Jon knew that Anthony was twenty-seven-years old and on the GI Bill. Jon also knew that he, Jonathan Adamson, was the only non-veteran St. Olaf freshman who would be assigned a room with a GI that fall.

"It's either four eighteen year olds in a room," his father had said, "or room with our one leftover GI, or else live at home. What will it be?"

"I'll take the GI," Jon had replied without hesitation. He'd seen some of the GIs on the campus and around town, especially the football team that had come in early. They were mature, confident, suave looking.

When his father had proposed the rooming situation, the pulp magazine ads flashed back through Jon's mind. Nothing he could imagine would mature him more quickly than rooming with a GI, a shortcut to impressing Rhonda Rasmussen.

Having offered Jon the choice, Dean Adamson then gave his son a brief sex and morality lecture. "GIs are older," he said, "and more experienced. . ."

As his father lectured, Jon's mind wandered. He would learn the ropes from his new roommate—how to dress, how to walk, and especially how to talk with girls. Jon imagined that just when classes were starting, Rhonda would at last notice Jonathan Adamson because he hung out with older guys. She would look intently upon him with full respect and adoration, and would love him as he loved her.

Jon climbed the remaining stairs, then headed down the hallway to room 223. He tried the door tentatively, knowing that if it wasn't open, he had a key. The door swung open slowly, and there, he guessed, stood his roommate, Anthony Tarpezi.

Jon first noticed the olive drab army underwear and then the body, all hair and muscle, two hundred pounds of it, he estimated.

Staring into a rectangular mirror attached to the back of an old oak chest of drawers, Anthony was, with some difficulty, trying to wrangle a comb through his reluctant black curls. Even from the side Jon could see this was a wounded man. The meaty muscle on his left arm bore a wicked A-shaped scar. The letter was far from scarlet. More like perch belly white.

Anthony turned and stared. "You the paperboy?" he asked and nodded at Jon's newspaper bag.

"I'm your roommate—I think."

"No shit? They gave me a paperboy for a roommate?"

"No, I'm Jonathan," he said. Jon reached out his right hand with feigned confidence, the sort of thin courage one might muster while stroking the head of a friend's pet skunk. "Just Jon is okay."

"I'm Tony," he said, ignoring Jon's outstretched hand. "Tony Tarpezi. They called me 'Tony the Torpedo' in North Africa." The outside of his right arm, from his knuckles to his elbow, was one continuous and knotty scar, as if it had been burned. Was that why he wouldn't shake hands, Jon wondered?

"That's where you were? In North Africa?" Jon was sure he looked wide-eyed and stupid. This was a bona fide war veteran. Tony had really been there, in the places Jon had only read about.

Tony didn't answer. He turned away and resumed tugging the comb through his curls.

Taking the cue to mind his own business, Jon slung his newspaper bag off his shoulder and onto the caned seat of an oak bentwood chair. He started unpacking.

He hoped sometime Tony would tell him his war stories. Starting in the early forties, Jon had ordered an extra daily and Sunday newspaper for himself. It cost only pennies at his newsboy wholesale price. He clipped out maps of land battles and sea battles, and hung them on his bedroom wall. He studied bombed-out towns in photographs. Jon planned to major in history at St. Olaf, and to teach history himself some day.

Tony cleared his throat with a wracking hollowness that made

Jon jump out of his reverie.

"Tank corps," Tony blurted an extremely delayed reply, pointing to the patch on the olive jacket hanging over his desk chair. "The Rommel Routers." He pulled his arm back with a slight abruptness, as if he didn't want his roommate to relate his all-too obvious wounds to a particular theater of war.

"That all you brought along?" he asked, pointing at the newspaper bag.

Jon nodded.

"Good. Then it'll take you about one second to unpack. I need help decorating this dump." He pointed to a pile of rolled-up posters and pinup pictures lying on his desk.

Tony pulled his top desk drawer open and yanked out a shoe box. Jon instantly thought of his Rhonda treasures. What does this guy collect? he wondered.

Tony opened the box and Jon saw that it contained tools. Tony pulled out a hammer and a small Mason jar half full of mixed nails.

"Pick out some of the small nails," he ordered, handing Jon the glass jar.

Jon carefully picked out the smallest nails and laid them on his desk. Tony began to hang the pictures, hammering the nails through the posters' upper corners. Jon gawked, conscious of his eyes growing wider and wider. He'd never seen such a collection of photos. Naked and near naked women, voluptuous women of all nationalities.

Tony had trouble raising his left arm above his shoulder. He handed Jon a poster, the hammer, and two nails.

"Up there," he said with a grunt and pointed.

"These are my Petty Girls," he said and waved at one set grouped together on the wall. Jon had already recognized them from his wartime reading. Artist Petty's bathing suit pinups.

Most of the pictures were hung now and the wall above Tony's desk was completely covered. Tony pointed to the few remaining rolled-up posters and asked, "Want some over your desk?"

"No," Jon said. "I wouldn't be able to concentrate on my studies, or anything."

"Ha," Tony said with a snort.

Jon felt his face grow hot. He sat down on his desk chair and risked saying, "You know they'll charge you for every nail hole."

"Screw them," Tony said. After musing on that a minute, Tony asked, "Who will?"

"The maintenance crew."

"How do you know that?"

"I work on the crew during the summer."

"You're from town?"

"Yes. I'm a 'townie.' And—you might as well know right off. My dad's the dean of men."

"You mean here? At this college?" Tony pointed both his index fingers at the floor like six shooters.

"Yes."

"Holy *whore's* feathers." Tony threw himself onto the lower bunk. He hooked the fingers of his right hand through the wire mesh spring that held the upper bunk mattress above his head, exposing his armpit. The hair under his arm looked like a muskrat pelt. "They put me in the same room with the frickin' dean's kid?"

Jon nodded.

"You s'posed to spy on me, or what?"

"No. My dad said there was an odd number of GI Billers and that you were the only one who didn't have a roommate. So I'm your roommate. My dad figured if it was me, at least it wouldn't be some P-K whose parents would complain."

"What the hell's a P-K?"

"A preacher's kid."

"You're telling me that the frickin' dean's kid is better than a preacher's kid?" Tony jumped to his feet, grabbed a handful of his olive boxer shorts, and rearranged his testicles. Like a languid jungle creature he meandered over to the open double-hung window and shrugged his butt.

"Just don't squeal on me, Jon Adamson. I plan on getting plenty of Norwegian tail in this monastery and I don't need any frickin' dean's kid looking over my shoulder."

"I won't spy. I won't squeal either," Jon said. "And I'll try to get used to having *frickin'* for a middle name."

Tony snorted again. He didn't sound amused.

Jon tried to envision what Tony the Torpedo might do to a Norwegian tail. The nearest thing to an erotic image he could summon up was long blond hair flowing like rivulets of sunshine over Tony's wild black curls.

The Norwegian tails had better watch out, he thought.

4

With St. Olaf's freshman class almost doubled in 1946, registration day, normally a trial, became an ordeal. The frustration was palpable. Partly because so many GIs were choosing courses in the sciences and in business administration, department heads had to scramble to enlarge sections, rearrange teaching times and make quick deals with part-time teachers, sometimes pressing the emeriti or emeritae back into service.

Jon watched the popular professors scratch their heads and sigh. Classes would be large and their work schedules even larger. When Jon walked by the sociology table, he heard Doc Sogge gesture toward a group of GIs and whisper to Professor Weisheit, "I'm glad the war is over, but teaching small classes of mostly girls was pretty nice the last few years." Weisheit smiled and nodded.

Jon was listed in the third registration group and Tony the fourth. By the time Jon's turn arrived and he was allowed inside the gym, much important registration news had already been recorded in columns on a large blackboard at the far end of the gymnasium.

To reach the tall blackboard and register changes, Miss Bergen, Assistant to the Registrar, stepped on a folding chair, then onto a table. Her well sculpted legs, sporting newly-available post-war nylons, caught the eyes of a group of GIs who whistled. Jon's father sidled over and whispered to them quietly. The whistling stopped, but the ogling didn't.

The blackboard listed courses in three columns:

SECTIONS CLOSED   SECTIONS RE-OPENED   NEW SECTIONS

Many of Miss Bergen's entries elicited groans from the crowd. Several confrontations occurred between disgruntled GIs— Anthony included—and the registrar, Miss Thorsgaard.

Jon knew Tony wanted to take biology but all biology sections had been listed on the blackboard as closed when Tony entered the gym with the fourth group. Jon watched Tony argue with Miss Thorsgaard about it. He knew Tony was doomed. Her Norwegian stubbornness was legendary. Miss Thorsgaard pointed to the philosophy department table. Tony marched over there, fuming.

Tony paced back and forth like an infuriated caged beast in front of the philosophy table. Finally he stoppped, grabbed a pen, and registered for a course. Jon cruised in alongside him.

"Are we going to be in the same philosophy section?" Jon asked.

"Fuckin' bitch," Tony spat, jerking his head at Miss Thorsgaard. "Philosophy." He shook his black curls in disgust. "Holy shit."

"Philosophy fulfills a graduation requirement," Jon said. "Did Miss Thorsgaard tell you that?"

"I *know* that. I can read, for God's sake," Tony said, snapping his catalog angrily with his index finger, which catapulted sharply off the ball of his thumb.

Tony stormed out of the gym, leaving Jon standing alone, hugging his catalog to his chest. Jon watched Tony walk through the crowded lobby and kick over a waste can on his way out the door which he slammed behind him. The floor was strewn with garbage. All the students standing in line stopped talking and stared after Tony, wide-eyed.

Jon was tempted to follow him out, but he saw Rhonda standing in line, waiting to register. He looked at his watch. He'd stay in the gym until her group was allowed in to register, a twenty minute wait. Could he kill that much time, he wondered, without being arrested for loitering? He'd sure try.

He got a drink from the corner fountain. He went to the rest room. He studied and re-studied the registration blackboard. He got another drink. He went to the rest room again.

Finally Rhonda's group filed in. Jon locked his eyes on her. She wore a grey blouse, a knee-length navy blue cotton skirt, white socks and brown loafers. Many girls in the gym were wearing such outfits. Somehow Rhonda made it look a hundred times better.

From a distance, Jon secretly followed Rhonda from table to table, trying to guess what her daily schedule would be. She left the speech and theater table and Jon casually strolled over and chatted with Professor Nelson. "That student who just registered," Jon said and pointed at Rhonda, trying to sound business-like. "Did she get the course she wanted?"

"If she wanted Introduction to Acting she did," he replied.

"Good," Jon said and smiled cordially. Later he'd look in his class schedule and see where and when Intro to Acting met. Jon planned to camp out in the hallways and in front of buildings wherever Rhonda's schedule took her. Sooner or later she'd notice him. Sooner or later she'd like him. One day soon she'd love him.

Jon followed Rhonda out of the gym. He watched from the front steps as she made lunch arrangements with a group of girls, then he followed them to the cafeteria.

Jon filled his tray and decided to eat alone. He knew he didn't have to. He saw a couple of other townies in the caf he could have joined. He didn't know them well. They were casual acquaintances from high school. Most of his closest friends had gone to other colleges. But he could have eaten with them. He also spied Tony sitting with some other GIs across the room. He didn't dare invite himself into that group—not yet. No, today Jon would eat alone, for one purpose—to watch Rhonda from the best vantage point.

He waited with his tray until Rhonda had chosen a table and

taken her seat, then he picked a place two tables away.

Jon slowly sipped his milk and munched his sandwich, barely taking his eyes off her. More than anything he wished he was sitting beside her, sharing a meal with her.

I wouldn't want to eat many meals alone like this, thought Jon, squirming in his chair. As his meal disappeared he began to feel uncomfortably conspicuous. It would be his first choice to eat with Rhonda. Second choice, Tony. Third choice, the other townies if he had to—only to avoid eating alone.

Jon knew—his older sister Trudy had told him all about it— that at St. Olaf being a townie was an advantage at first. Jon figured the first couple weeks were probably torture at any college, a conspicuously lonely hell and ordeal in isolation, especially at mealtimes. Most freshmen were probably thankful for their assigned roommates at mealtimes. They'd sit with them no matter how odd they were, thought Jon. A roommate was *somebody* —and that was better than nobody. Better to be with a zipper-faced Frankenstein's Monster or The Hunchback of N.D. (North Dakota) than to eat alone.

It seemed Jon couldn't count on Tony for culinary companionship. Not yet anyway. Tony had left their room for meals all week, ignoring Jon, not even telling him where he was going, much less inviting him along.

Would he regret his decision to room with the one leftover GI? Jon wondered.

Jon's sister Trudy had told him that breakfast was the most common meal to eat alone. That made it the worst meal of the day. There were always empty spaces so kids could—and usually had to—sit alone in the mornings, each table like a desert island with one inhabitant. Half the kids didn't even eat breakfast, Trudy said, which, for those who did, made the emptiness and loneliness seem even worse. Jon figured a really shy kid might skip a lot of meals to avoid sitting alone.

Lunches were better, Trudy maintained, suppers best. The place was packed in the evenings. The islands were full. Students had to sit shoulder to shoulder. They asked questions. They made small talk. When there were only a few chairs available, no one had to choose between loneliness and starvation.

Jon made his fruit cup last forever so he could study Rhonda as long as possible. She ate with the same grace with which she did everything. She chatted easily with her classmates, was physical in conversation—pushing shoulders, gesturing, popping the heel of her hand off her temple to show astonishment. She was, to Jon, in every little way, and in every big way, absolutely beautiful.

Suddenly their eyes met. For the briefest second Rhonda's brown eyes met Jon's. She flashed a half smile, but it was the bakery smile again, the be cordial to customers smile.

Maybe if I sat with Tony and the other GIs, Jon thought, I'd look older and more mature, then Rhonda would notice me. Jon vowed he'd scrape up the courage to invite himself to supper with Tony. Today.

After lunch Jon bought his books and supplies at the bookstore. He went to a couple of orientation meetings, then returned to room 223 late in the afternoon. Tony and another guy sat comfortably slumped in the desk chairs, drinking whiskey and water.

"This is Jon, my roommate," mumbled Tony. "This is Flyboy, air force vet."

"Want one?" Flyboy asked Jon, holding up his cup of whiskey.

"No. No, thanks," Jon said. He moved around Flyboy and tried to appear busy by arranging his new books and supplies on his desk top. Finally he dropped his materials and sat down on the lower bunk, edging himself into the little group by aiming his body inward.

The three sat in silence for a minute. Flyboy sipped his drink. Tony gulped his. Jon tried to wind up enough courage to mention supper.

Flyboy nodded at Tony then turned and asked Jon, "So what's it like rooming with a grizzly bear?"

Tony gave Flyboy a wry, half smile, then watched for Jon's

answer. Jon thought quickly. He'd spent almost a week with Tony. A roommate who barely talked. Who barked orders when he did. Who didn't include his roommate at mealtimes. Who drank liquor like a sponge. Who thrashed around in his sleep so obviously and loudly disturbed that he kept Jon awake.

"It's an education," Jon finally said.

"That's what we're here for," Flyboy said and chuckled.

Tony poured himself another drink.

"That's your fourth," Flyboy said. "We'd better go eat supper right now or you won't be able to walk."

"Mind your own fuckin' business," Tony said to Flyboy, with neither anger nor malice in his voice.

"Well, Jon and I are going over to eat," Flyboy said, nodding to Jon. "If you want to sit here and drink yourself shit-headed, okay—but I say it's time for the three of us to go eat."

Tony gulped down his drink and stood up. He thrust his hairy arms into a shirt and was still struggling with the buttons when they got to the central stairway.

Flyboy stopped. "Tuck that shirt in your pants," he said. "You look like a bum."

Jon couldn't believe how Flyboy gave Tony orders and got away with it. Must be the military training, Jon thought. Tony had been a tank corporal. From his wartime reading Jon knew all pilots like Flyboy were officers, lieutenants or better.

As they walked out of the dorm Jon marveled at his luck. They were on their way to eat. He'd stumbled into an invitation. Just what he wanted and he hadn't even had to ask.

Eating with these GIs, Jon soon learned, was a perplexing mental zigzag between embarrassment and intrigue. Flyboy was fairly easy. He chatted freely. But Tony ate swiftly, silently and sloppily, military style, then "chick-checked," as he called it, while he gulped his coffee.

Tony watched every female student walk by with her tray, his head twisting like an owl's.

"Geez, what knockers," he muttered. "Cute little ass."

One of his observations was enigmatic: "She'd be beautiful if she weren't so ugly."

Flyboy joined in the sport, though he was gentler.

"Those three should be welded together," he said, nodding toward a group of girls. "Her face," he said and pointed, wiggling his finger at each girl in turn, "with her legs—with her beautiful gluteus."

"With her headlights," Tony added, pointing at another student, then cupping his hands graphically six inches in front of his chest. Before anyone had a chance to react he turned to Flyboy and asked, "What the hell's a gluteus?"

Jon cringed. He was sure that kids three tables deep could hear Tony's crude observations and see his lewd gestures. He was also sure that Tony's four stiff shots of whiskey were having their effect.

Jon worried that a girl might hear the remarks, especially a girl from one of his classes or a girl he knew from town.

Suddenly Rhonda entered the caf. Jon noticed her being noticed. Hers was not a subtle beauty. He watched her furtively, hoping Tony wouldn't see her. Attempting distraction he blurted, "Did you guys get any good classes?"

"I did okay," Flyboy said.

"Not me," Tony said with a grunt, then muttered "fuckin' bitch" under his breath.

No one said a word for a full minute.

"The problem," Tony finally said, "was that my alphabetical group registered next to last. No matter what group registers first next semester, I'm going to be in there."

"How?" Jon asked.

"Sneak in."

"But *how*?"

"I'll figure out a way." As an additional exclamation mark, Tony delivered a not too gentle right cross to Jon's shoulder. It hurt a little, but Jon appreciated the gesture. Enemies never slugged each other playfully on the shoulder.

Tony became pensive then, scooping at the bottom of his soup bowl for the last translucent pearled barley pellet. Suddenly he looked up. His eyes widened.

"Holy balls," he whispered. "Who's that?"

Jon had never before heard Tony whisper. Although he knew exactly who Tony had seen, he didn't dare look. He'd dreaded this moment. He ignored Tony's question. Tony the Torpedo, Jon decided suddenly, protectively, could ask someone else about Rhonda Rasmussen. He sure wasn't volunteering.

Let Tony ask someone else about the impossible odds against a full-blooded Norwegian having jet black hair and autumn oak leaf colored eyes and fawn tan skin and hands that moved like a ballerina's.

Let some other townie tell him that Rhonda's sister and her husband owned the Northfield Bakery and that Rhonda had worked there for three summers and all the previous year, saving money for college.

Let Tony the Torpedo spend a year learning all that for himself—if he could.

5

It was one of the hottest Septembers on record. Radio forecasts
predicted continued sizzling temperatures and high humidity
throughout the first week of classes. Crowding and other incon-
veniences on campus set tempers on edge.

After his first day of classes, Jon, like most St. Olaf students,
went to his room after supper, picked up the books and assignment sheets he needed, then found a place to study in the library
reading room. He wandered around until he spied Rhonda, but
the study tables near her were all full.

He had to sit five tables away from her.

He got up several times on pretenses and walked past her
table. He inhaled deeply as he sailed past, trying to catch a whiff
of her sweet scent.

Like everyone else, Jon stayed in the reading room until it
closed at ten o'clock. About 9:45 students in the room began to get
noisy and restless. He watched intently as students made eye contact or whispered plans to meet in the Lion's Den—the campus
coffee shop on the library's underground level. A few brave males
sidled over to girls and suggested coffee or Coke dates. Those with
both courage and a little money suggested burgers and malts.

Jon ached to walk over and invite Rhonda to the Den. He
willed his feet to get up and move, to carry him over to his beloved
Rhonda.

His feet ignored him.

Jon decided he'd build up more courage and ask her soon—maybe even tomorrow night.

Weeknight Coke dates for freshman women were a hurried affair anyway, Jon knew that much. The library closed at ten o'clock and the doors in Agnes Mellby Hall were locked at 10:45 sharp on weekdays.

Men and women who lived off campus had no curfew, Jon knew that also. When the crowd thinned in the Den at night, they walked off the Hill to their rooms in private homes or to the military Quonset huts below Old Main. A bus took men who didn't have cars to their Springbrook Farm chickenhouse dormitory.

Jon waited until Rhonda had gathered her books and purse, then followed her out of the library. On the sidewalk she was swallowed up in a group of girls who headed back to Mellby Hall. Jon turned away and returned to his own dorm room.

He found Tony sitting languidly at his desk, wearing only his underwear, and staring at a textbook.

"Was it this hot on the desert?" Jon asked.

A long pause, then Tony replied, "Hotter."

"It must have been terrible inside a tank."

"We sweat a lot. Salt pills helped." There was another long pause. It was obvious that Tony didn't want to talk. "I gotta read this shit," he finally said.

Jon took the hint. He wanted so badly to ask about Tobruk or El Alamein, battles in North Africa and Egypt he'd read about.

Jon wound his alarm clock, then stripped for bed. He took his history book with him to the top bunk to read a few more pages. He had no idea where his study hours were going to come from. For just the first week he had seventy-five pages assigned in philosophy, forty in religion, and half of Book I of Ole Rolvaag's novel *Giants in the Earth* for English.

From where he lay on the top bunk, Jon could comfortably spy on his roommate from the back. Tony's hairy shoulders were beaded with sweat. Jon studied the burly muscles, the scar, the burns, the way Tony's sweaty fingers stuck to the pages of his text-book.

Jon also noticed that Tony wasn't just studying. Jon watched him fill his enameled tin cup half full, then raise it to his lips and drink deeply.

Suddenly, at eleven o'clock, the lights flicked off.

"What the *hell*," bellowed Tony. "Turn the damn lights back on, Jon."

"I didn't turn them off."

"Well, who did?"

"The whole campus goes dark at eleven o'clock. They told us that at the men's orientation lecture, the one you and Flyboy and the others skipped last week."

Tony fumbled in his desk drawer for a flashlight and turned it on. He tugged on his tan trousers and hopped to the door, zipping his fly with one hand and holding the flashlight with the other as he disappeared down the hall.

Jon lay in bed for ten minutes, silent and awake, until Tony returned. Tony wasn't alone. The flashlight's beam darted around the room. Several men spoke in hushed voices.

"Wake up, Jon," Tony hissed.

"I'm not asleep."

In the semi-darkness Jon recognized several of Tony's GI friends.

"Get up, Peckerson," Boomer barked. "Tony said you used to live in this dump when you were a kid. So where's the light switch?"

"Down in the basement," Jon said. He kicked his legs over the side of the upper bunk and sat up. "Are you going to turn the lights back on?"

"You bet," Boomer said. "No fuckin' geek of a resident head like that Tenner Tullingson asshole is going to turn the lights off on me." He sounded drunk, and smelled like it too.

"Show us where the power room is, would you, Jon?" Flyboy

asked in a gentler voice.

"Okay. Let me just get my jeans on."

The delegation shuffled to the center stairwell, down to the main floor landing, then down past the back door to the underground level. The hallways were lighted, but all other lights were out.

Jon led the group halfway down the basement hallway to the room where all the pipes and wires entered through a tunnel from the power plant. A metal sign screwed to the front of the door said, POWER ROOM.

"If any of you shitheads could read," Boomer drawled drunkenly, "we could have found this ourselves."

Tony tried the door knob. It was locked.

"Anyone got a paper clip or a piece of wire?" he asked. "I'm pretty good at locks." No one had any wire, so they fanned out along the hallway searching for a makeshift tool. No luck.

"This is stupid," Boomer shouted.

"Shut up you loud-mouthed idiot," Tony snarled. "Tullingson will hear you."

"So what are we going to do?" Greasemonkey asked with a giggle. "Wish it open like Dorothy?" His hands over his face, he spun in a circle and chanted in a falsetto voice, "There's no place like home. There's no place like home."

"Shut up with that stupid shit," Boomer slurred loudly. "Everybody move back. I'm going to open this goddam door."

Boomer cocked his right knee back against his chest, then suddenly fired out with his right foot. He had no shoes on. His bare foot struck the door just beside the knob. The door exploded open. Wood chips flew back and struck several members of the delegation.

"Yow!" Boomer yelled, dancing around on his left foot. He collapsed on the floor, grabbing the bleeding toes of his right foot.

The others stepped over him and into the power room, ignoring Boomer's writhing. Jon remained in the doorway, too nervous to take full part in the sortie.

"Which switches?" Greasemonkey asked. "There's a whole wall full of switches."

They all turned to Jon.

"That box there," Jon said, pointing. "There are about fifty switches."

"You better go back to your room," Flyboy whispered to Jon. "The dean's kid shouldn't be in on this."

"Flyboy's right," Tony said, cocking a thumb toward the stairwell. "Get the hell out of here."

"Let there be light!" Jon heard Greasemonkey shout and giggle maniacally. Shark, Tony, and Flyboy joined him in turning on dozens of switches. Jon thought he heard Flyboy humming "This Little Light of Mine," but shook it off as improbable.

Flyboy suddenly noticed that Jon was still there, watching.

"Get him out of here," Flyboy said to Shark. Shark took two steps over to Jon, turned him by the shoulders, walked him into the hall, then gave him a gentle push toward the center stairwell.

Boomer continued to groan, sitting on the floor. He leaned against the hallway wall, his right foot cradled in both hands, his face twisted in pain.

Shark glanced at Boomer and laughed. "Boomer, you idiot," Shark said. "If you weren't so fuckin' drunk all the time, maybe you wouldn't be so stupid."

They were all talking so loudly by then that Jon was sure they'd get caught. Besides, lights suddenly going on all over the dorm were bound to attract attention.

Fearing probation or even suspension, Jon turned and started to run up the basement stairs. At the first floor landing, he spotted movement to his left. He turned and saw the resident head, Tenner Tullingson, in his bathrobe, hurrying toward the stairwell.

Jon flew back down the stairs, three steps at a time. He dived under the staircase and crawled back into the shadows. After Tullingson had padded down the steps, Jon crawled partway out to watch. He had a clear view of the power room door.

"All right. What's this all about?" Tullingson whispered in the sneering voice that Jon knew many students had learned to hate.

"I broke my damn foot, that's what," Boomer said with a loud groan.

"That's right," Shark said, smothering a snicker.

"These lights are going back off," Tullingson said, his eyes glaring.

"No, they're not," Tony announced. He stepped squarely in front of Tullingson and put his hands on his hips defiantly.

"I second that motion," Shark said, stepping up at Tony's left side.

"I third it," Flyboy said, stepping up at Tony's right.

Jon knew Tullingson was no match for them. No single man would have taken on those three vets, especially with Boomer's ghastly panting as background music. Tullingson certainly wasn't man enough. Jon knew he'd back down.

"We'll just see about that," Tullingson said. He turned on his heels so quickly that Jon dived back into his hiding place, bumping his head.

Jon returned to his room ten minutes later. He had waited several minutes after everything quieted down before daring to creep out of the crawl space.

"Where were you?" Tony asked from his desk, without turning around.

"I was telling a couple of guys on the main floor what you did." That was the truth, but Jon would never have admitted to hiding in the crawl space. "They say they're going to call you guys The Light Brigade."

"No shit," Tony said. He sounded bored and tired.

Boomer hobbled around campus in the days that followed. He was fined twenty-five dollars for wrecking the door, but several other GIs kicked in a few dollars each to help out. Once again, Uncle Sam paid the bill.

From that day forward, the lights in Ytterboe Hall stayed on, day and night.

6

School had barely started and Jon was already swamped with reading assignments, essays, and speeches. Indoors and out, temperatures still sizzled.

Although autumn is usually Minnesota's most pleasant season, there is occasionally an equatorial day. But September, 1946, had dozens of scorchers strung together, breaking all existing high temperature records. Minnesotans endured ninety degrees and higher both day and night. The humidity was high, the air uncomfortably sticky. It was far worse than a typical July. Even the faintest breezes seemed, like gossip, to issue from no discernable direction. Sleep was next to impossible.

Classrooms were stiflingly hot. Many professors just shrugged, gave students reading assignments, announced a few pertinent items, then dismissed classes. Never once had that happened to Jon in high school. At Northfield High School students were dismissed when the bell rang and not before.

Somehow the heat seemed at its worst in room 223. Jon lay there sweating night after night in that breezeless room, remembering summer nights when he'd slept in the breezy screen porch at home. He'd lie there comfortably and fondly listen to Northfield's night sounds—steam and diesel trains in the distance, the midnight shift whistle at the Malt-O-Meal plant, Bubby Weed's motorcycle.

In room 223 the only night sounds came from his roommate. Tony managed to fall asleep in spite of the heat but slept fitfully. Jon often lay awake listening as Tony groaned and cried out and took deep, distraught, and panting breaths in his sleep.

What on earth had happened to Tony overseas in the war? Jon wondered.

Sometimes, Jon regretted having been too young to go to war. He felt a kind of Miniver Cheevy born too lateness, a Don Quixote nostalgia for the glory of it all.

Jon and his friends did what they could. They collected scrap metal, rubber, and paper. The drives were usually organized by schools or Boy Scout troops. Scrap metal and paper sometimes grew to mountains in schoolyards, all to alleviate critical wartime shortages.

Every American family did its part for the war effort, living with rationing—gas, tires, food, especially butter and sugar—but that was a minor inconvenience, an insignificant homefront sacrifice. When Jon listened to Tony's frenetic dreams, and saw the scars on his arms and the haunted look in his eyes, he was thankful he'd been too young to fight.

As the September nights grew even hotter, sleep became more impossible, even for Tony. On Sunday night, after Jon and Tony had lain awake for more than an hour sweating and unable to sleep, Jon walked across the hall in his jockey shorts and knocked on the door.

He heard a shuffle inside, then the door swung open. Three roommates popped their heads into the doorway like a trio of rabbits in a Bugs Bunny cartoon.

"Hi," one said.

"Hi," Jon replied. "Hot, isn't it?"

"Beastly," said the spokesman. The other two nodded.

Prep school, Jon thought, hearing his nasal tone and British word choice. La-de-da.

"It struck me, ya know," Jon said, trying perversely to sound as public school as possible, "that a breeze might have a chance of blowing through if we both left our doors open. See where our windows are?" he added and pointed, "and where yours is?"

The threesome moved a few inches beyond their doorframe to look. What they saw over his shoulder, Jon was suddenly aware, was not the open windows but Tony sitting at his desk in his army underwear with a backdrop of pinups on the wall. Maybe they also spied Tony's several tattoos or the jagged scar winding its way across his arm like the white belly of a garter snake. No doubt they also saw the virile black curls poofing out from Tony's armpits and the mat of wild hair running all the way down his back and disappearing in his olive drab boxer shorts.

Undoubtedly this trio was aware of Tony's newfound campus reputation—kicking over the garbage can on registration day, a yelling match with Shark in the hallway one night, a couple of noisy re-entries after late nights in Dundas bars.

Jon saw distrust and fear in their eyes. The spokesman shook his head and the trio backed into their room and shut the door in Jon's face. Jon knew the door across the hall would be locked tight all night, probably all term, and that Tony and Jon would have neither breezes nor invitations to high tea from their commonwealth neighbors.

Jon marched down the hall to the bathroom before turning in. Living with Tony is isolating me, isn't it? he asked himself as he splashed cold water on his face and chest, trying to cool off. He stared at his dripping face in the mirror. Living with Tony is definitely skewing my social life, he thought. Those guys across the hall are my age, freshmen too. But I'm not one of them. Rooming with Tony has changed that.

Jon felt tall as he strolled in his underwear back to room 223. He felt older and somehow more mysterious. A better match, he thought with satisfaction, for the beautiful Rhonda.

Wednesday was the hottest night yet. There was no breeze at all. The air was suffocating. Neither Jon nor Tony could sleep so they studied instead, in silence.

"Enough of this shit," Tony finally said after midnight. "I'm sleeping outside."

"Too many mosquitoes on the lawn," Jon said.

"Somewhere high then," Tony responded, "up where the stonemasons are working on Thorson Hall. Or maybe climb up the ski jump scaffold." Tony thought a minute, then asked, "Were you around this summer when they painted that gazebo thing on the roof?"

"Yup."

"Did the painters use ladders—or a scaffold?"

"I don't remember any ladders or scaffolding."

"Then there must be a trap door."

This was the most Tony had spoken to Jon since they met. Jon's heart skipped a beat at the breakthrough.

"It's in the attic," Jon said. "I've seen it."

"How do you get to the attic?"

"There's a door at the top of the center stairwell."

"Any idea what kind of lock is on the door?"

"I remember it's an old fashioned keyhole. The kind they peek through in Laurel and Hardy movies."

"Ach zo," Tony replied in Nazi, raising his eyebrows. He pulled a pliers and flashlight out of his desk drawer and grabbed a coat hanger off the wall hook. Using the pliers, he snipped the wire into several short pieces. He bent a loop on one end of each piece and miniature L-shapes on the other end. In three minutes he held several tiny homemade wire keys in his hand.

Tony slipped the keys' loops over his little finger, picked up his flask, pillow, and a sheet, and left the room without a word.

Jon jumped up. He grabbed his pillow and sheet and ran after Tony. "Can I come?" he asked.

Tony shrugged. "If you want," he mumbled.

Clad only in underwear, they padded softly down the hallway in their bare feet, Jon tagging along behind Tony like a puppy. Flyboy popped out of his door as they passed and punched Tony's pillow.

"Going to a slumber party, Tincan Man?" Flyboy asked and smirked.

"Up your bomb bay, Flyboy."

Jon followed Tony to the center stairs, up two flights to the third floor, then up two more flights. The topmost set of stairs ended abruptly at a five-panel door.

There was no landing, just a door in the wall. Tony stood on the top step, Jon two steps below. Tony dropped his pillow and sheet at his side, set his silver flask carefully on top of the pillow, and handed Jon the flashlight.

Tony slid one of the three little keys off his finger. Jon shined the light at the door as Tony shoved the bent wire key into the keyhole. He wiggled it deftly, then tried to turn it. Nothing.

Tony tried a different key. Still nothing.

"Shit," he muttered.

The third key worked. The lock clicked back, and Tony swung the door open slowly, quietly.

"That didn't take long," Jon whispered. He shuddered then. The compartment of his conscience which reminded Jon that he was the dean's son now warned him he could get in trouble doing this. Could he even get kicked out of school? he wondered. I don't care, thought Jon with a half smile. He envisioned himself one day walking across campus with Rhonda, pointing to Ytterboe's cupola and saying, "Last September when it was so hot I slept up there."

"*Really,*" Jon could hear her saying, astonishment and admiration in her eyes.

Jon and Tony stopped inside the attic and Tony eased the door shut silently. He took the flashlight from Jon and quickly, methodically looked around. Jon could imagine him in uniform, his rifle at ready, making similar moves in a bombed out building.

Tony studied the attic, careful to keep the beam from flashing across the tall dormer windows. Piles of broken chairs, chests with missing drawers, stacks of mattresses and army blankets filled the musty room. The far end of the attic housed discarded backdrops and sets from the college theater. Jon recognized castle walls from

Macbeth and a large seascape from *The Odyssey,* draped with real fishnets.

Tony cast the beam up at the open rafters. They were several inches thick and at least fourteen inches wide. Each was a perfect piece of lumber, white pine, probably, from trees like those Jon's Norwegian grandfather had lumberjacked north of Bemidji. Because the roof was so steep, the rafters were very long. Thirty, thirty-five feet maybe. Jon tried to imagine a forest of trees that straight and tall.

"They don't make buildings like this anymore," Jon said, resting his hand on the nearest rafter.

"I know," Tony replied. "Back in Italy we blew the shit out of lots of nice old buildings like this."

"You were in Italy, too?" Jon whispered.

"After Africa. Then they shipped our tanks across the Mediterranean and we started fighting our way up the boot." Tony paused and aimed the flashlight at Jon's face. "I thought you were Mr. History Know it All."

Jon shrugged, trying to hide his delight that Tony was finally talking a little. "I knew that army divisions went from North Africa to Italy," he replied, "but I didn't know yours did."

"That's where I got hit," Tony said and tapped the flashlight on his left arm making the beam shudder across the dark floor. "Speaking of hit, I need to hit the sack."

"Right."

Tony threw one of the army blankets over his shoulder. Jon did the same. Tony put his flask in his teeth, then led the way up the ladder. Jon followed, his nose just inches away from Tony's hairy calves. Jon was sure Tony's calves had a larger circumference than his own thighs.

Twenty feet above the attic floor, Tony pushed up the hinged lid of the trap door, carefully lowering it to the floor of the cupola so it wouldn't bang. They climbed through the hole and onto the cupola's tin floor which glowed in the light of a magnificent half moon. They spread their blankets and sheets on the floor and lay on their backs, their heads on their pillows. Tony sat up again, walked on his knees over to the trap door, and lowered it back over the hole.

"This better stay closed," he said. "I sometimes sleepwalk."

"Oh," said Jon. We're nearly a hundred feet off the ground on a puny platform with no railings, he thought, and this wounded vet tells me he sleepwalks. Okay. Well.

"Calm down," Tony said, obviously noticing Jon's concerned look. "Nothing will happen. Go to sleep."

Jon obeyed. A breeze wafted over his bare chest, the first hint of coolness he'd felt in days. Exhausted after several nights of little sleep, Jon drifted off in seconds.

Rumbles of thunder awakened Jon hours later. He had no idea what time it was, but the moon was very low. He sat up on his blanket. Lightning flashed across the southern horizon.

He rolled over for a better view of the sky and counted the seconds between flash and crash. He figured the storm was five or six miles south, just past the town of Dundas. Spectacular bolts of varying intensities illuminated their sleeping quarters on the cupola. The thunder rumbled, subdued but insistent.

"They're shelling us again, Captain," Tony mumbled in his sleep. He sat up on his blanket, still asleep, and stared southward toward the lighting.

Suddenly a bright bolt of lightning and a sharp clap of thunder caused Tony to explode to his feet.

"No," he cried and screamed. "Watch out." He dropped to his knees and yelled, "We're hit bad, Captain. Come on. Let's get out of here."

Crawling on his bare knees, Tony scrambled off the blanket and onto the cupola's tin floor.

I bet that tin feels like the steel floor of a tank cockpit, Jon thought anxiously. Should I wake him? Jon had read somewhere that waking people out of nightmares wasn't smart.

"I'll help you get your leg free, Captain," Tony shouted, "then I'll push you out of the cockpit. Roll over," and mumbled on. "Roll over, Captain. You can do it." Tony tugged at the phantom captain with his right arm, straining mightily and finally succeeding in the maneuver.

Suddenly Tony screamed. "Oh, Jesus, captain," he cried. "Jesus. Your whole chest's gone. I can see your heart beating, for God's sake." He tugged desperately on the invisible captain's body.

"We're burning, Captain. We've got to get out. You've got to help me get your leg free, Captain. My arm's hurt."

Then Tony leaped crazily and screeched, "I'm on fire." He slapped wildly at his right arm with his left hand.

"This can's going up, Captain. I gotta get out. I'm sorry to leave you, Captain. I'm so sorry," Tony whispered in the saddest voice Jon had ever heard in his whole life.

Tony bolted toward the cupola's edge.

Ytterboe Hall's roof was as steep as a Swiss ski jump. If Tony went over, Jon knew he'd slide helplessly down the steep roof, headfirst, then down three and a half stories to the concrete sidewalk below. Tony stood poised with one hand grasping a round pillar, looking like he just might step out into space.

Jon knew, instinctively, that if Tony stepped off the tin platform and Jon tried grabbing him, that Jon's own 145 pounds couldn't possibly pull Tony's two hundred pounds back onto the cupola. More likely they'd both go over the edge. Geez.

Jon quickly slid to his knees, wrapped his left arm around the pillar and thrust his right arm between Tony's legs. He reached his right hand beyond the pillar and locked it over his left wrist like a boxcar hitch. He clamped Tony's left thigh tightly against the pillar. Jon locked his chin behind the pillar too, for extra leverage. He prayed that the wooden pillar hadn't spent its lonely half century in snow and rain rotting away up there.

"Wake up," Jon hollered. "For God's sake, Tony, wake up."

The old pillar held—and so did the thigh lock.

But Tony didn't move.

After what felt like hours, Tony put his left hand on the pillar and pushed himself back from the cupola's edge. He stood unmoving then, but Jon didn't dare let go.

"It's okay, Jon," Tony said.

"You sure?"

"Just let me go."

Jon released his wrist grip cautiously. Tony turned around and stared down at Jon in the semi-darkness.

"Vat's going on up dere?" a voice shouted from below.

Tony dropped to his knees beside Jon and they both crept noiselessly to the center of the platform.

Jon recognized the thick Norwegian accent. It was Helge, the campus cop. A few times during Jon's junior and senior high school years, Helge had kicked Jon and his friends out of the college gym and off dormitory fire escapes.

Jon was ready to shout back and identify himself—to tell Helge not to worry—when Tony clamped his hand over Jon's mouth. Tony bisected his lips with his index finger, making the universal shush sign.

Helge must have thought the commotion was coming from one of Ytterboe's third floor dorm rooms. "Yust keep it down," he shouted and walked on.

Tony and Jon sank back down onto their blankets. They sat there in silence for a long time. Jon's skinny torso accentuated Tony's massive shoulders and chest, his hard muscular body magnified by every sliver of blue light from the moon and stars above and by the distant and fading flashes of golden lightning. Tony looked like a larger than life statue of a wounded Roman god cast in bronze.

The thunder finally diminished to a whisper, then stopped. Jon noticed the glow of dawn appearing in the east. Tony flipped the trap door back and dropped the blankets and pillows through the hole.

He took a long slug from his flask, replaced the lid, clamped the flask in his teeth, then climbed down the ladder. Jon followed him, pulling the lid closed above him and lowering it into place with his head.

Back on the attic floor, Jon scanned the space. What a great hideout it would be, he thought—chairs, mattresses, blankets. He wanted a key of his own, a skeleton key maybe.

Tony relocked the attic door with his makeshift key, then laid the key on top of the doorframe. "The key's there if you ever need it—and only you and I will know it's there," Tony said. "Don't tell anyone else."

When they reached the lighted third floor landing, Tony stopped abruptly and gazed directly at Jon. It was the first time since they'd met that Tony's round brown eyes had looked squarely into Jon's.

"You want to find yourself another roommate?" Tony asked.

Jon shook his head. "No," he said. "No, I don't."

Tony nodded slowly.

"You could have been killed up there," Jon said.

"I know," Tony replied. "I owe you one."

Tony's burned right arm reached out and squeezed Jon's skinny shoulder. Tony's arm quickly fell back to his side. He turned and they walked in silence, shoulder to shoulder, back to their room.

7

"You going to the *First Nighter* tonight?" Jon asked on the Saturday evening after their Wednesday on the roof.

"What's that?" said Tony.

"Haven't you seen the posters? It's a party for the freshman class. They pair each guy off with a girl for the night."

"For all night?" Tony asked.

"Not *all* night," Jon said with a smirk.

"And no drinking? And no dancing? This school doesn't know how to party. Not interested," Tony said with a grunt. He grabbed his hat, slipped his flask into his back pocket, and was off to his usual GI Saturday night downtown.

Jon arrived at the First Nighter ten minutes late, on purpose. His sister Trudy had told him how guys and girls were paired off for First Nighter dates. Jon knew if he was a few minutes late he'd have a better chance of getting paired off with Rhonda.

The system for pairing was obvious to Jon the minute he stepped into the gym lobby. Two lines snaked across the basket-ball floor from the entrance—girls in one line, boys in the other. Trudy had said each couple would be introduced at a table in the middle of the gym floor.

Jon ran up the side stairs and onto the second level running track that encircled the gym at its periphery. Hiding in the shadows, he quickly scanned the girls' line.

Where was she? he wondered. He looked for her shiny black hair and the familiar curves of her shoulders. He finally spotted her in line and began counting frantically. She was the forty-first girl in line.

Jon quickly counted off forty boys and memorized the freckled face of the tall redhead he absolutely had to stand behind. He ducked back down the stairs and walked nonchalantly across the basketball floor. Jon quietly struck up a conversation with the redhead. He laughed and nudged the boy's skinny shoulder, then squeezed his way into the line behind him.

Jon was forty-first in the boys' line. Rhonda was forty-first in the girls'.

Proud of his keen trickery, Jon thought of the evening ahead with nervous exhilaration. Rhonda Rasmussen for the whole night. Oh boy.

He kept sneaking glances at her. It seemed everyone in line was counting down now, gawking across the gym floor. Some counted very obviously, giggling and pointing index fingers, then smiling shyly at their counterparts on the opposite side of the gym. Jon saw one paired couple point at each other simultaneously from across the room, laugh loudly and call, "*You?*"

Rhonda just stood there carefree, chatting with her neighbor. She never looked across the room. She didn't count at all.

The moment Jon noticed Rhonda's supreme maturity, he followed suit. He abruptly stopped sneaking glances at her and stood smiling at the freckled neck ahead of him, waiting patiently.

Several upperclassmen and women standing at the table busily paired off couples and introduced them. Each minute Jon took several steps closer to the table, forcing himself with pure willpower not to look at the girls' line.

Suddenly he was beside the table and face to face with a short blond girl. Cute. Bright-eyed. Smiling. But not Rhonda.

Rhonda. Where was *Rhonda?* Jon whirled around and saw her strolling off with the tall guy who had stood in front of him in line.

Jon had counted wrong. He was one off! How could he have

counted wrong? He had always gotten As in math.

Jon stared at his date and managed a weak smile. She was a solid little green-eyed girl. She was pretty, and she had a nice friendly smile—but she wasn't Rhonda.

An upper class host introduced Jon to his date. Her name was Holly Hanson. She was from the lake country in northern Wisconsin.

An upper class hostess led Jon and Holly across the floor to a group of three other couples. The eight were assigned to be together, to spend at least part of the evening as a group.

Jon bit his lip, trying to hide a grin and his giddiness. The lovely Rhonda was in his group of eight.

When everyone had been paired, an upper class host on stage gave directions for a name charade.

"You have to act out your partner's name," he shouted, and laid out several rules. "Because so many of you are Norwegians with last names like Olson, Johnson, and Larson, you can pretend to rock a baby to make Ole into Olson and so on."

Jon acted out Holly's name by humming "The Holly and the Ivy." Then he held up one hand. Then he rocked the invisible baby. "Hand-son," Rhonda's date, the tall skinny guy, guessed right away. "Holly Hand-son."

Jim, Rhonda's date, had trouble acting out Rhonda's name. No one had a clue. He pretended to be using a file, and Jon secretly guessed it right—a rasp—for Rasmussen. But Jon obeyed the rules. He already knew Rhonda's name and all players had been instructed to follow this strict rule: If you already knew the person's name you were forbidden to play that round.

The hostess pointed to Rhonda at last and said, "Is there any-one in the group who hasn't been introduced to this girl, and who isn't in one of her classes or in her dorm—but who knows her name?"

Jon hesitated only a second. "Rhonda Rasmussen," he said.

Rhonda looked at Jon quizzically and so did Holly.

Jon, Holly, Rhonda, and the other five in their group remained together for the rest of the party. They played more games and watched upper class students act out skits up on stage that poked fun at St. Olaf life. Everyone drank punch, munched cookies, and ate cheese and crackers.

Jon knew Tony would've been bored to death. He'd have judged this First Nighter party to be as bland as oatmeal and Mission orange pop. Will rooming with Tony sour me on the simple stuff I've always enjoyed, Jon asked himself, like playing balloon volleyball in the church basement with the Luther League, stuff like that? Jon guessed maybe so.

Jon surreptitiously studied Rhonda all evening. She seemed to be bored with her date, Jim, but was polite and tolerant of him.

Suddenly Rhonda turned and grabbed Jon's arm gently. His heart almost leaped out of his chest. "How did you know my name?" she asked.

"I've seen you at the bakery," he admitted quietly, his heart thumping loudly.

"You're from Northf—?"

"Okay, Frosh. Listen carefully," the host boomed from stage. He shouted rules for a new game. All conversations in the room ceased while everyone listened.

Jon was in anguish. He and Rhonda had actually been talking. He wanted to talk with her forever. He wanted to be with her forever. The only reason he'd come to the First Nighter at all was to see her.

Everything in Jon's whole life suddenly seemed so childish and tame—the First Nighter included. Wednesday night on the cupola, although it was just the residue of excitement for Tony, had certainly been the most exciting night in Jon's life to date. Looking around at the party, Jon agreed with Tony. Cookies and games and skits didn't add up to big thrills. Not compared to cupola nightmare adventures. Jon was growing infuriatingly impatient with this party. He didn't want to go through all this to get a date with Rhonda. He wanted a shortcut to her company. And he wanted it now.

The party wound down and everyone gathered in clusters outside the gym. The other two couples in their group of eight strolled away and Jon, Holly, Rhonda, and Jim stood together.

"I've got to leave now," Rhonda said. "I'm spending the night downtown at the bakery. My sister needs help in the morning decorating cakes."

"It's after ten," Jon said. "That's pretty late to walk downtown alone." Holly nodded but Rhonda just shrugged. "I could walk you down if you like," he offered.

"But you were paired up with Holly," Rhonda said with a mock frown. "You should walk *her* back to the dorm."

"Would you mind?" Jon turned and asked Holly. "She shouldn't walk down there by herself."

"It's okay," Holly said, although her tone suggested that it wasn't entirely okay.

"I'll walk you back to your dorm," Jim said to Holly.

Holly smiled reluctantly.

Jim was obviously relieved. All night anyone who watched him could see that being with a girl as beautiful as Rhonda was uncomfortable for him. Jon was sure that Holly was more Jim's style, more the June Allyson type. Wholesome. The girl next door. Jim might even try kissing Holly goodnight. Jim would never risk touching Rhonda, Jon was certain of that. But Jon felt a growing confidence surging up in his own veins. He would risk it soon, kissing Rhonda. Oh, he couldn't wait.

After saying goodbye to Holly and Jim, Jon and Rhonda walked in silence down the path past Old Main. Two blocks beyond Old Main, Jon pointed to 918 West Second Street.

"That's my house," he said.

Rhonda just smiled.

After a long pause, Rhonda asked, "Why do you look so familiar? It seems like I've seen you before—and not just once, but many times."

Jon bit his lip, wondering what to say.

A smile broke across Rhonda's face that looked astonishingly beautiful in the golden light of the street lamps.

"You've been watching me," she said softly. "Haven't you?"

Jon nodded.

"Why?"

His head swam. He wanted to say, Because you're the most beautiful woman I've ever seen.

"Well?" Rhonda demanded with a slight frown.

Then out it came. "Because you're the most beautiful woman I've ever seen."

"You know," she said, smiling, "I thought it was something like that." She stopped walking then, turned to Jon and said, "Do you really think I'm beautiful?"

Jon nodded.

Rhonda smiled again, then turned and resumed her brisk walk toward mainstreet.

They walked the remaining eight blocks in silence.

On Division Street, Rhonda opened the bakery's front door with a key she kept on a chain around her neck. She pulled the key out from between her breasts, bent over and unlocked the door without taking the chain off. With a wave she invited Jon to follow her inside the entryway, then she bent over again and locked the door behind them.

"Slide into that corner booth back there," she said, nodding toward it. "I have to call upstairs—let my sister know we're here— then I'll get you something. What'll it be? A malt maybe—or the best cherry Coke of your life?"

"I'll take the Coke," Jon said. He was thrilled that Rhonda hadn't just thanked him at the front door and sent him back up the Hill. She'd actually invited him inside the bakery. All the previous year he had dreamed of such a moment. He couldn't believe this was happening to him.

Jon slipped into the booth and watched people strolling past the shop window. They couldn't see him seated back inside the dark bakery. It was fun, kind of like spying. He saw several people he knew. One woman puckered her lips and applied fresh lipstick, using the window for a mirror. She didn't see Jon back in the shadows. He felt a sense of power, being able to watch and yet remain unseen.

Rhonda hung up the phone, then moved over to the soda fountain. Jon turned sideways in the booth to watch her at the counter. She spurted dark dashes of Coke and cherry syrup into two glasses. "Ice?" she asked.

"Just a little." Oh, what joy.

"Sure. Do you want a doughnut or a cookie? Or I could make you a sandwich. The bread is great."

"No. No, thanks," Jon said with a slight squeak in his voice. "Just the Coke." He knew he'd never be able to choke down food in his nervous state.

She slipped in opposite him in the back booth and handed him his drink. There they sat, just a table width apart, sipping their Cokes. What ecstasy.

"You're right," he looked up and said, "This *is* the best cherry Coke I've ever had."

Jon couldn't take his eyes off of her. She swirled the Coke around in her glass with her straw, rattling the ice quietly.

"So you think I'm beautiful?" she asked.

"Yes," Jon said. "Yes, I do. And you sing beautifully too."

"You've heard me sing?"

"Yes. In *The Wizard of Oz*."

"Well. You *have* been watching me."

She didn't seem displeased. In fact, she seemed tickled, even touched. She smiled across the booth at him and Jon's confidence soared. He chose the candid approach.

"Last Easter break I drove up and cruised past your house," he admitted.

"You mean in Edina?"

"Yes."

"You drove way up to Edina just to see me? Jon, that's the absolute sweetest thing I've ever heard," she said. Her smile, long after the fact, made every mile to Edina the previous spring worth the trip.

Suddenly the phone rang. Rhonda jumped over to the counter and grabbed the phone from its cradle. She whispered into the receiver for a minute, then returned to Jon's side.

"That was just my sister upstairs," she said. "I have to go up right now."

Jon jumped to his feet and started to follow Rhonda, then ran back and carried the Coke glasses to the counter.

"You *are* sweet," she said.

He followed her through the kitchen and work room to the bakery's back door. She drew back the latch and opened the door for him. Jon stepped out into the alley and Rhonda studied him, her lovely head at a thoughtful tilt.

"Your eyes are light blue," Rhonda said, "like a lake."

Jon grinned. He was in heaven.

"Do you know, your eyes are so light blue they're like mirrors. I can actually see myself in your eyes—two tiny Rhondas, one in each eye. Isn't that *extraordinary*, Jonathan?"

She was beautiful beyond description. Jon was speechless. And he absolutely loved the way she said his full name— *Jonathan. Jon-a-than.*

She leaned forward. Jon thought she was going to kiss him. Instead, with her right hand she raised the key that hung on the chain around her neck and dragged the cool metal gently across his cheek.

"Thanks for walking me home," she whispered, dropping the key back between her breasts and slowly closing the door.

Jon stood there alone, enraptured, for a full minute. The Cannon River rippled audibly on the far side of the parking lot. Jon turned and floated back to Manitou Heights.

Jon stopped outside his dorm room door and rubbed his cheek, musing on Rhonda's golden key. He took a deep contented breath, then strolled inside.

Tony sat at his desk reading his history text, his tin army cup half full of whiskey, the nearly empty bottle standing boldly on his desk.

"Want some?" he asked, pointing to the bottle. Jon shook his head and yawned, trying to hide his smile and pleasure at Tony's overture of friendship. Their night on the roof had changed their relationship. Jon sensed it, and he was sure Tony did too.

"So how was it?" Tony asked, swiveling halfway around in his chair, turning his back on his history book.

"The First Nighter? Not too exciting. Okay though," Jon said. He considered telling Tony about Rhonda and the bakery, maybe by doing so registering her as his find, his property.

Before he could speak, Tony suddenly took a big gulp of whiskey, then cleared his throat and spoke.

"One of those girls I saw in the caf last week. . ."

"Yeah?"

"The pretty one with the long black hair. . ."

"Yeah?" Jon knew he sounded like a trained parrot.

"She's in my freshman composition class," Tony said. "Do you know her? I found out she spent last year here in Northfield."

Jon managed a nonchalant shrug. He knew Tony was talking about his cherry Coke angel, the dream woman who had just tickled his cheek with the key to her heart.

"What's her name?" Jon finally asked in a whisper.

"Rhonda Rasmussen," Tony the Torpedo said, filling the room with a piercing wolf whistle. Damn.

8

Now that Tony knows Rhonda's name, Jon thought, as he lay awake in the night listening to his roommate's nocturnal whimpers, he'll be after her. When he sees her in the caf, he'll walk right over and sit at her table.

In the morning, Jon got dressed quietly and left his still snoring roommate and hiked down to St. John's for the early service. He sat in the balcony and scarcely paid attention to the lessons or the sermon. How, he asked himself, could he keep Tony and Rhonda apart?

After the service, back in his room, Jon managed a "hello" when Tony appeared from his morning shower, clad only in a towel. He held his toothbrush in his mouth, gumming the bristles.

"Maybe that Rhonda will be at lunch today," murmured Tony, talking through the bristles. "Maybe I'll just saunter over and plop down on her lap." Tony smirked and the toothbrush fell from his lips. He caught it deftly with his left hand then winced, even from that minor strain of his arm.

No, thought Jon, I can't let this happen.

Suddenly he blurted, "Hey, Tony, want to go have lunch in the cities?"

"You mean hitchhike?"

"No, in my car."

"You've got a car? Since when? You never said you had a car."

"I keep it at home. Other townies have cars at home."

"So what does the DEAN say about that?" Tony asked in a sonorous voice dripping in sarcasm. "I thought cars on campus were against the *rooooooles?*"

"I obey the rules," Jon said. "I keep the car off campus. But driving to the cities on a weekend would be okay."

"Yeah," Tony said, bobbing his head of curls. "Yeah. More than okay. I've asked Flyboy a dozen times to borrow his car. He won't let anyone drive it."

"He might let me drive it," Jon said, teasing his roommate.

"Why would he?"

"Because I don't drink."

Tony laughed, then said, "Boy, getting out of this shit hole would be great. And not just for lunch—the whole afternoon. So when do we leave?"

"Now."

"I'll buy the gas. Minneapolis, St. Paul, Twin Cities, here we come," said Tony, jumping into his clothes and grabbing his flask.

They walked down to 918 West Second Street and into the garage. Tony laughed out loud when he saw Jon's Model A Ford roadster.

"I thought you said you had a car," he said and hooted again.

Jon's mother must have heard the laugh because she stepped out to the garage just then. Jon introduced them.

"Hold on a minute," she said and smiled at Tony. "I just made some cookies."

They drove west out of town on Highway 19, munching cookies. Jon glanced over at Tony. He was smiling. Jon had seen him smirk before, but never smile.

Tony washed down his cookie with a long slug from his flask. Then he did something even more unexpected than smile. He began to hum. Jon kept his eyes firmly glued on the road ahead, trying to appear nonchalant as his roommate displayed this rare good mood. Tony actually hummed two complete traveling songs, start to finish: "In My Merry Oldsmobile" and "Come Josephine in My Flying Machine."

Tony had a deep resonant voice. He hummed beautifully, and right on pitch. Jon's sister Trudy had taught Jon a lot about voices. If Trudy heard Tony hum, Jon knew she'd suggest he try out for the St. Olaf Choir.

The little roadster also hummed along. At September's mid-point, the hot weather had broken, but the days remained pleasantly warm. As Jon turned north on Highway 65, the warm sunny day and the freedom turned Tony downright chatty.

"A Model A is your basic car," he said, running his fingertips over the pressed steel dashboard.

"Yup," Jon agreed. He patted the shaped sheet of metal that served as the instrument panel and also part of the hood and the back wall of the gas tank. The windshield was fastened to it as well. "All cars," Jon added, "should be so multi-purposed and simple."

"What year is it?"

"A '29."

"What'd it cost you?"

"Fifty. I had to put a radiator on it, though, and two tires."

"It's not your ideal picking up girls car."

"I suppose not," Jon agreed. He reached across and adjusted the carburetor needle valve to highway speed.

"If this crate were a Buick or even a DeSoto, and if you didn't look so much like high school, we could pick up some women in Minneapolis. I could show you how a whore can field-strip herself under her coat, right out on a busy street, and no one would even notice."

Jon grimaced at being labeled "high school." What would it take, he wondered, for me to appear older, wiser, more worldly—to Tony—and to Rhonda?

"That so," Jon said, trying to visualize the field-stripping, and not sure he'd even want to see that. He thought of Rhonda suddenly and, in spite of the warm wind whistling through the car, felt chills run down his neck.

They drove along silently through the rolling pasture land over the nearly deserted highway.

"So," Jon finally asked. "What *could* we do in a Model A Ford?"

"I don't know," Tony said. "A movie maybe? Flyboy told me there was a place called The Alvin Burlesque—vaudeville and a floor show with dancing girls—"

"Look. Up ahead," Jon interrupted him, taking one hand off the wheel to point. A police car's flashing red light a hundred yards ahead made Jon brake the roadster suddenly. He slowed the car to a crawl.

"Pull over," Tony ordered.

Jon pulled the roadster to the shoulder and stopped.

An old pre-war Plymouth lay on its side in the ditch. Two policemen squatted and peered through the windshield.

Tony jumped out of the roadster and loped toward the overturned Plymouth. Jon suddenly thought about the war. What Tony must have seen overseas, Jon thought with a shudder. Not only his tank captain, but others—comrades, friends, enemies, bleeding, torn up, dying.

Jon stepped out of the roadster and stood there motionless. He remembered reading a story about a GI whose legs had been blown off just above the knees in a marine assault. There he was, that GI, helpless on the beach, the stumps of his legs and his hands stuck in the sand, a midget suddenly, who looked with terrified eyes at everyone who ran by until his life's blood had drained away into the beach beneath him. Then he tipped over dead.

That scene had appeared several times in Jon's own nightmares.

He had never seen anything worse than a five stitch cut.

From an insulating distance, Jon watched Tony drop to his knees beside the policeman.

"He's breathing," Tony said to the officer. "Better leave him for the ambulance."

The policeman nodded.

"But the other one's bleeding pretty bad," Tony said and pointed. "We'd better get him out."

Tony vaulted up and stood on the side of the overturned car with his feet wide apart on the rear door. He yanked the dented front door open. A teenage boy wobbled to his feet in the open doorway then collapsed over the car body. His face was badly cut. Blood covered his face and the entire front of his shirt.

Tony and the policeman worked together to pull the boy out. He was dead weight, in and out of consciousness, and hefty too. Tony grimaced as he strained at the weight with his own wounded arm. He and the policeman finally succeeded in dragging the boy out of the car and laid him in the weeds.

Tony dropped beside the boy and grabbed the tail of his own button-down shirt. He ripped the side panel out of his shirt and folded the cloth into a compress. With his thumb and forefinger he carefully pressed together the deep cut on the teenager's face, then applied the compress. Tony pressed hard. Blood oozed out of the cloth and between his fingers. He held the compress for ten interminable minutes—talking quietly to the boy who moaned each time he slipped back into consciousness—until the ambulance arrived.

The ambulance screeched to a stop and when an attendant's hand replaced Tony's on the compress, Tony stood up.

"Let's *go*," he snapped and yanked Jon's arm roughly.

Back in the roadster, Jon waited to turn on the ignition. Tony sat staring at his hands. They were dripping in blood.

"Got a rag?" Tony asked.

Jon shook his head.

Tony ripped the other side off his button-down shirt. "God I hate blood," he mumbled, wiping his hands on the cloth and throwing it on the floor. "It's so sticky."

The cloth had been ineffectual in ridding Tony's hands of the bright red blood. Tony continued to stare at his hands.

"What now?" Jon asked.

Tony didn't reply.

"We could stop at a store in Minneapolis and buy you a new shirt."

"Head back," Tony said.

Tony didn't say a word the whole way back to campus. It was complete silence for more than twenty minutes, Tony staring at his bloody hands the entire way. At the final bend in the road on Highway 19, Tony suddenly doubled over, his head falling onto his knees. He began to shake uncontrollably.

Jon pulled over, the four-cylinder engine throbbing at idle. "Tony?" he asked. He didn't dare reach over and touch him.

Tony finally stopped shaking. He sat up straight. He didn't look at Jon, just nodded for Jon to get moving.

Jon put the car in gear, let out the clutch, and pulled back on the highway.

Jon drove his car on campus—against the strict school rules that applied to freshmen and dropped Tony off in the loading area behind Ytterboe Hall.

"I have to take the car home," Jon said quietly. "I'll see you later."

Tony didn't say a word. He didn't look at Jon. He stepped out and clicked the door shut.

Jon watched Tony walk away. His shoulders hunched, Tony struggled across the loading lot like an old, old man.

Back in his parents' garage, Jon cleaned the blood from his car door and dashboard with a pailful of water and a rag. He was thorough in the task and felt like a criminal trying to remove evidence.

He wiped smears off the door handle and drops off the floor. Finally finished, he tossed the bloody water onto the grass. He picked the wad of bloody shirt cloth off the car's running board and jammed it deep in his parents' garbage can so no one would ever see it.

He turned and stared at his little car. He wiped some dust off the fender with his finger. He knew he should be getting back to school—but felt reluctant to return to room 223 and to Tony.

The sun was setting over the west edge of the campus as Jon walked back up the Hill. The place was nearly deserted. The after supper crowd was already back in dorm rooms or at the library.

As Jon walked toward Ytterboe, he impulsively turned into the stairway that led down to the post office on the basement level of the library. He decided to check his PO box and maybe read a few notices on the bulletin board, postponing as long as possible his reunion with Tony.

Outside his dorm room door at last, Jon stopped to consider what sort of entry to make.

There are so many ways of entering a room, he thought. You can ease your head in, whisper a tentative and questioning hello. Or you can strut in with a big hi, plant yourself there, and wait for some response. Or you can walk in, businesslike, and barely acknowledge the other occupants of the room.

Rooming with an enigma like Tony, Jon had no idea how his troubled roommate would want him to enter tonight. So Jon simply took a deep breath and turned the knob.

The door was locked.

They'd never locked the door before, neither Tony nor Jon. They'd never needed to, since Tony's presence was a lock of sorts. No one would mess with Tony Tarpezi's door. His doorknob would never be smeared with jam or toothpaste. His door would never be pennyed shut. No one would ever dare prop a wastebasket full of water against Tony's door in the middle of the night. Not with Tony inside. Jon had himself an around the clock personal bodyguard.

Jon gently rattled the door. He knocked softly at first, then with more urgency.

Was Tony all right? he wondered.

"Who is it?" Tony finally called from the other side of the door. His voice sounded garbled.

"It's me, Tony. Open up."

Jon heard a chair skitter across the floor, then tip over. Tony slammed the lock back loudly, then swung the door open.

He stood in the doorway, completely naked. Gee.

And he was drunk.

"Hi, Peckerhead," he shouted. "Where ya been?"

"Get inside," Jon ordered, pushing Tony back through the open door and using his foot to slam the door behind them.

"Run around drunk and naked and yelling your head off and you'll get kicked out of school," Jon said, shaking his head.

"You goinnnna squeeeal toooo *Daddeee?*" Tony shanked every syllable in the numb chambers of his mouth, his breath a tincture that seemed to sterilize every pore in Jon's face.

"I won't *have* to squeal if you keep on yelling," Jon said. He marched across the room and picked up the overturned bentwood chair, leaving Tony teetering in the center of the floor.

Back with the chair, he sat Tony onto the seat, not daring to smirk as he imagined for a second the scotch plaid pattern the caned seat would leave on Tony's bare butt.

He stepped back to consider his next move, and Jon noticed that Tony's hands were still smeared with dried blood.

Jon studied Tony, whose head was bobbing down to his chest. He looked like he'd topple off the chair at any second.

Knowing he wouldn't be able to lift him off the floor, Jon quickly darted behind the chair, grabbed the seat frame, and dragged the chair over beside the bed. He pushed Tony's shoulders and lowered him onto the bottom bunk. He rolled him onto his back and lifted his legs up.

Tony was out cold. Before covering him with an army blanket, Jon studied Tony's naked body and sneaked a look at his penis. Ooh.

Tony's cock was a serious apparatus, hardly diminutive enough to be called a pecker. His was a cock, no doubt about it. Jon hadn't witnessed a penis that size since he'd seen his father's friend Professor Johnsrud skinny-dipping in Smith Lake.

Jon covered Tony with the army blanket, then sat down in the chair and stared at his huge, unpredictable, disturbed roommate. Had it been a mistake rooming with him?

In the last ten minutes Jon had managed to sound tough and

in control. But on the inside he felt jittery with fear and apprehension. Drunks and emotional misfits were new entries in his life. Everyone he had ever known acted normally, predictably.

Jon noticed Tony's left hand hanging out of the blanket. Jon decided Tony shouldn't have to wake up and look at those gory hands again.

He stepped over to his desk and quietly dumped the pens and pencils out of his Land-O-Lakes butter crock. He stared for a moment at the familiar trademark on the crock, a kneeling Indian princess.

Jon looked closely at the princess. She looked amazingly like Rhonda. Rhonda. She was the impetus for taking today's road trip in the first place. Jon had almost forgotten. Well, he'd figure out a way to keep Tony and Rhonda apart, at least until he had won her over.

Jon turned away from the crock and looked at Tony again. He remembered Rhonda dragging that cold key across his cheek at the bakery door. She saw herself in my eyes, Jon thought. My blue eyes. She belongs with me, not with a drunken hairy ape like Tony. He's no competition, thought Jon with a confident smile. He leaned over and kissed the princess on the crock. His lovely princess Rhonda, kneeling, submissive, so very beautiful.

Jon carried the crock to the bathroom at the end of the hall. He returned with the crock full of steaming water. Not wanting to stain his own clothes, Jon stripped off his tee shirt. He set the crock on the chair seat, then bent over and began to wash Tony's left hand gently with a washcloth.

Jon finished and reached for Tony's right hand. Suddenly Tony opened his eyes. He studied Jon's bare and skinny upper body and mumbled, "You got pretty small tits for a nurse."

His lids closed again instantly and he began to snore.

Jon gently washed Tony's right hand. The water turned bright pink. Blood clots that stuck to the washcloth became bright red spots on the white terry cloth. Reconstituted blood, thought Jon. Like the new frozen orange juices and instant coffees the stores were selling. Just add water.

Back in the bathroom, Jon rinsed out the crock. He wadded up the bloody washcloth and threw it with all his might straight down into the empty trash can. The thump seemed to echo off the tile walls.

Jon returned to his room and kissed the princess again, then put the pens and pencils back in the crock. He checked Tony's breathing, crawled into the upper bunk and fell into a fitful sleep, dreaming of Rhonda, war, and blood. Strange.

9

Monday morning Jon woke at dawn. The room reeked. It smelled just like fermented silage. Jon climbed down from his bunk and opened both windows to air out the place.

He stared at his snoring roommate. Tony had so much liquor in his system that he'd probably sleep through his 8:50 class. Jon grabbed his wind-up alarm clock and nested it in Tony's pillow next to his ear, hoping that would wake him.

Jon showered, dressed, and gathered up the books he needed for class, then headed to the caf for breakfast. One advantage of Tony's drinking sprees, thought Jon as he kicked through a sea of autumn leaves en route to the caf, is that he usually sleeps through breakfast. That meant one less mealtime for Tony to "chick-check" Rhonda.

At the caf, Jon filled his tray and spotted Rhonda sitting at a table with Holly. They know me now, Jon said to himself. I can invite myself to sit with them. A cinch. Courage. Courage.

He moved toward their table. Before they even saw him, Rhonda suddenly stood up, said goodbye to Holly, and left the caf behind an upper class boy wearing a letterman's jacket.

"Hi, Jon," Holly said brightly. "Were you going to join us?"

"Yes."

"Well you could join *me*, anyway," she said, motioning to a chair across the table from her. "You like Rhonda, don't you?" she

72

asked when Jon had settled into his chair.

"Well, yeah, sure, I guess," Jon stammered.

"No one has ever looked at me the way you look at her."

Jon's face burned. He bent over his tray and concentrated fiercely on buttering his toast.

After a few uncomfortable moments, they began to chat superficially, then both of them got up, picked up their trays, and left for their 8:50 classes.

Jon took the long way around to Old Main, detouring past the Music Hall. He knew Rhonda had to be there for her 8:50 class. He saw her on the steps, talking with the same upper class boy she'd followed out of the caf. Something the boy said made Rhonda throw back her head and laugh.

What am I going to do? Jon thought with a groan. I really have to get her to notice me somehow.

Jon stopped back at the room after chapel to grab a couple more books. Tony was gone, but his bed was made, neatly. Jon gave the army credit for that.

Suddenly the door banged open. Tony breezed in and Jon heard a clink as Tony laid a paper bag carefully in his drawer. He grunted a hello.

"Did you get to your 8:50 class?" Jon asked.

"Naw. I hitchhiked downtown to buy something," he said. "Hey, what does it mean in this town when people put furniture and stuff out by the curb?"

"You mean like mattresses and old chairs, things like that?"

"Yeah," Tony said and nodded.

"Must be Rummage Week," Jon said. "Twice a year people put junk out and the town sends trucks to haul it all to the dump."

"Can anyone take that stuff?"

"Sure. Guys with pickups scour the whole town during Rummage Week. I got a toboggan that way once. Still have it."

"I could use some help," Tony said. "I saw something down on the curb that I want."

"What?"

"My ticket into the best classes at next semester's registration."

"Meaning?"

"Just come on. You'll see."

As they walked down the Hill without saying anything, Jon wondered how Tony's head felt after all that alcohol. Neither of them mentioned the car accident or its bloody aftermath. Jon figured they probably never would.

The elms were beautiful, their leaves now yellow gold. The autumn sunshine carved light sculptures in the gothic arch that formed over the street by the gradual rise of the tree limbs. Squirrels leaped from branch to branch above the street in the golden, leafy canopy.

Jon studied the glowing mosaic as they walked down St. Olaf Avenue. He was willing to bet that Tony had never seen a town as beautiful as Northfield. The trees were huge and the building lots wide and well kept. It was a rare house that wasn't painted white or stuccoed natural gray.

This is what Tony was fighting for, thought Jon, a walk on a sunny autumn day in a quiet town with big, old elm trees, a town that hadn't been blown to slivers by bombs and shells.

They walked three blocks down St. Olaf Avenue. Junk was piled along the curb in front of most houses.

"There it is," Tony said and pointed.

Jon saw a pile of residue from a remodeling project: plaster and lath, nail-studded molding, tar paper, and several old plumbing fixtures.

"*What?*" Jon asked.

"There," Tony said and pointed at an old toilet.

"That's your ticket to the best classes next registration?"

"Yup."

"How?"

"Trust me."

"A toilet? And you say trust me? Next semester's registration is three months away. What are you going to do with a toilet until then?" Jon asked with a laugh.

A smirk crept onto Tony's face, hiding the ashen color of his hangover for a moment. Jon was delighted that they were talking—even about a toilet—and that Tony seemed to be in good humor.

"Keep it in our room," he said. "Use it for an extra chair. Give me your puny knife for a second."

Tony used Jon's penknife to cut sash cords from a smashed window frame, then tied a loop through the bolt holes behind the seat on the porcelain toilet.

"The tank, too?" Jon asked, pointing.

"We don't need the tank," Tony said. "Just the seat."

"It won't flush."

"It won't need to. Shut up and just help, will you."

Tony slid a two-by-four through the rope loop. The two of them squatted, nursed the two-by-four onto their shoulders, and stood up. They trudged back toward the campus. The prize toilet swung between them like a trophy from a boar hunt.

Two blocks from the campus, Tony stopped the procession and said, "Hey, I want this, too." With the toe of his boot he gently tapped a small potted tree among a pile of castoffs on the curb.

"Looks dead to me," Jon said.

"It's not dead."

"A tree can't look much deader than that," Jon insisted.

"It's alive. I want it."

"What do you want a dead tree for?"

"It's not dead!" Tony said and snorted. He ran his thumbnail over one of the dry buds.

"If it's not already dead, it's on its deathbed," Jon said, flashing a grin at Tony.

Tony smirked and shrugged. He squatted down, careful not to let the two-by-four slip off his shoulder. He grabbed the pot with his left arm and fitted it onto his hip. Jon could see the extra weight hurt his wounded arm.

"Set it down," Jon said. "I'll get it."

They both squatted and Jon hoisted the potted tree and cradled it in his right arm. He and Tony headed back up St. Olaf Avenue with the tree and the toilet.

At the head of St. Olaf Avenue, a friend of Jon's father, a Carleton professor, stuck his head out his car window.

"I say, Jon," he called, "are they finally getting rid of the outhouses at St. Olaf?"

On the sidewalk outside the library, Jon and Tony were pummeled with wisecracks. That didn't bother Jon, but carrying the toilet up Ytterboe's stairs did. Tony couldn't raise his left arm above his shoulder, so Jon had to lift the two-by-four over his head so the underslung toilet would clear the steps. Jon knew that if the toilet slid down the board, the sash cord rigging would slice off his fingers.

Sweating and out of breath, they finally reached their room and set the toilet down in the corner. Tony pulled a couple of small boards from his back pocket and slipped them under the flange to steady the toilet.

"I still don't see how a toilet will help at registration," said Jon as he stood up.

"I'll tell you when the time comes."

"Okay," Jon said, feeling deflated and knowing he'd better back off.

"When word gets out that we have a toilet in here," Tony added, "Boomer or some other idiot will stagger in at midnight and piss on our floor."

"Better not," Jon said, very pleased that Tony was still talking and joking. "And here's your dead tree." Jon set the pot on Tony's desk.

"It just needs water," Tony said.

"It needs a miracle," Jon said and laughed.

Tony bent over and fingered a dry leaf on the tree. Then he straightened up and walked out the door without a word.

Jon watched Tony go and shook his head, thoroughly puzzled. One minute Tony's joking, Jon thought, the next he's out of here like I have chicken pox.

Jon shrugged and sat down to read his history text. A half hour later Tony walked in. He was actually grinning.

"Look," he said. He reached outside the door and slid in a small wooden tub inscribed with the words, "Lutefisk—Bergen." Inside the tub were two small bags of potting soil and fertilizer, and a gallon jug of water.

"How did you carry all that?" Jon asked, nodding at Tony's left arm.

"I set it down a few times."

"Where'd you get it?" Jon asked.

"I got the dirt and the fertilizer from John Berntsen down at the shop," he said triumphantly. "The tub and the jug of water came from Mrs. Turnbull over in the caf kitchen. All I had to do was say you were my roommate."

Jon couldn't believe how much Tony was talking, and how excitedly.

Tony and Jon repotted the little tree together, then set it on the toilet seat.

"You want to go eat?" Jon asked tentatively after they'd swept up the soil and stuffed the empty fertilizer and potting soil bags into Jon's wastebasket. Jon had no idea if it was acceptable yet that he extend a mealtime invitation to Tony.

"We can go after I water the tree," Tony said.

Jon felt victorious, a foot taller. Tony has accepted me, he thought. Next, Rhonda.

Jon had forgotten about Rhonda when he invited Tony to lunch just now. After going to so much trouble to keep Tony out of the caf, now they were heading there together. Jon walked confidently nevertheless, kicking through the leaves. She has to choose me, he told himself. My destiny.

There wasn't much of a line at the caf. Tony and Jon filled their trays and because it was still early, sat at an empty table. They'd barely started to eat when Tony shoved Jon's shoulder and said, "There she is. You sure you don't know her?"

Jon turned and looked over his shoulder. "I've seen her," he confessed. So cool, he would be.

"Hey, Rhonda," Tony shouted, so loud that heads turned and kids stared. "Come and eat with us. Bring your friend."

Jon turned again and saw that Rhonda was with Holly.

Rhonda stared at Tony as if she was seeing him for the first time. Perhaps she was, Jon thought. She noticed Jon then and smiled. Jon smiled back and waved them over. He sat straight in his caf chair, determined to maneuver all interactions in his own favor.

Jon jumped up and pulled out the chair next to him. He gently took Rhonda by the elbow and guided her into the chair. Holly moved to the other side of the table and sat by Tony.

"Holly, Rhonda, this is my roommate, Tony Tarpezi," Jon said, pointing at Tony. "Tony, this is Rhonda Rasmussen and Holly Johnson."

"Hanson," Holly corrected him.

"Sorry," he said to Holly. He turned to Tony and asked, "I guess you're in Rhonda's English class, right?"

"You are?" Rhonda said, tilting her head and studying Tony.

"I sit behind you," Tony said.

Rhonda's sudden curiosity about Tony made Jon slump a bit. He forced himself to sit up tall in his chair again. He quickly said to Holly in an attempt to steer the conversation down a different avenue, "You and Rhonda seem to have hit it off."

"We live only five rooms apart in Agnes Mellby Hall," Holly said. "Rhonda took me down to the bakery Saturday morning. We sat in back with her brother-in-law and ate doughnuts right out of the machine. I think I ate six."

Jon smiled.

"I'll be a blimp," she added, glancing down at her stomach.

"Naw," Jon said. "You probably walked them off going down there and back."

"I hope so," Holly said, smiling prettily at Jon.

"Funny I've never noticed you," Rhonda said to Tony. "Your

curls make you look like a dark cupid."

"Yeah," Holly said and laughed. "All he needs is wings."

"No wings on Tony Tarpezi," Jon blurted, not giving Tony a chance to reply. Everyone laughed.

Jon regretted having pulled Rhonda in beside him. She continued to stare intently across the table at Tony. If she'd sat across from me, Jon thought, she'd be gazing into my lake blue eyes.

"Why don't all four of us go down to the bakery Saturday night?" Rhonda suggested, pulling her eyes away from Tony and looking at the others. "My sister and her husband will be gone for the night."

Holly shrugged and said, "Sounds fun."

"Sounds great," Jon agreed and smiled at Rhonda.

"It's settled then," Rhonda said, returning Jon's smile. "Are you in too, Tony?"

"Sure," he said and nodded. "Can we use your car?" he asked Jon. "Maybe we could go to a movie first."

"Sure," Jon said.

"You have a car?" Rhonda asked Jon, her eyes wide.

"Wait till you see it," Tony said. "Right out of a Laurel and Hardy movie."

Rhonda laughed, her gaze settling again on Tony's black curls. It wasn't just Tony's curls and Jon knew it. Tony was interesting in so many ways. But Rhonda somehow had to see the massive differences between them and choose him, Jon. Jon the stable one, Jon the one with the blue, mirror-like eyes. Tony was after Norwegian tail and Jon didn't want his Rhonda to be part of the smorgasbord.

Rhonda looked at her watch and jumped up. "I have to go," she said. "I have a practice room for an hour. Choir tryouts are next Monday."

"Can't wait until Saturday," Holly said to her.

"Neither can I," Rhonda said. She patted Jon's shoulder and smiled at everyone.

Jon breathed deeply, savoring the lingering tingles on his right shoulder.

Rhonda grabbed her tray and quickly asked, "Are any of you going to try out for the choir?"

"Not I," Jon said, desperately wishing for the first time in his life that he had taken Trudy's advice and developed his voice. "My sister Trudy sang in the St. Olaf Choir all four years." He hoped that would impress Rhonda, but it was Holly who spoke next.

"I only sing in the shower," she said.

"I do that, too," Tony said to Holly. He raised and lowered his eyebrows like Groucho Marx and picked up a spoon, brandishing it like the famous Groucho cigar. "How about a wet duet sometime?"

Holly laughed and blushed.

"Did you ever sing in a choir?" she asked Tony.

"I sang in the boys' choir in my grandma's church for about four years," he said and smirked. "Until the priest caught me with the communion wine."

"Try out on Monday," Rhonda urged. "Sign-up sheets are in the music hall." She tossed her hair over her shoulder and hurried toward the kitchen wall, to the hole with work-study elves behind it, the hole that absorbed dishes, silverware, and trays like a magic vacuum.

Disquieting images suddenly filled Jon's mind. Visions of both Rhonda and Tony getting into the choir. Pictures of Tony and Rhonda spending two weeks together on tour the following spring. Two weeks in the back of a bus. Two weeks in roadside cafes. Two weeks in dark backstages of auditoriums. Two weeks in basement dressing rooms in churches. Two *minutes* in those churches' deserted furnace rooms. Too much.

Jon watched Rhonda swish toward the caf doors, her silky hair sweeping across her shoulders. Her upper body scarcely moved as she clamped her books against her beautiful chest. Only her legs moved—and her hips. And how. Oh those hips. Fluid drive.

Rhonda walked away from them, proud and erect. Oh, how Jon loved her.

10

"What's the movie downtown?" Holly asked as they stood around Jon's roadster on Saturday night.

"I don't know," Jon replied as he unsnapped the roadster's canvas top, "but we can go look."

Rhonda ran her hand over the red front fender and the teardrop headlight mounted above it. Holly tapped the toe of her saddle shoe on the spoked wheel, then hopped on the running-board. She bounced up and down, squealing.

"Hey," Jon said with mock sharpness. Her bouncing made unsnapping the canvas top more difficult.

Tony opened the passenger door. He pulled a small package out of his jacket pocket and slipped it under the front seat.

Jon folded the canvas top down, then swung the trunk lid back. He hoped Rhonda wouldn't hear his stomach growling. He had been too nervous to eat supper.

"There's a seat in there," Holly said with another excited squeal.

"It's called a rumble seat," Jon explained.

Tony grabbed Holly under her arms and boosted her over the back fender and into the rumble seat. She laughed, tossing her blond hair and arching her back, kicking her legs into the rumble seat cockpit like an Olympic gymnast. She didn't seem to notice that Tony's fingertips were pressed into the sides of her breasts.

Jon couldn't help noticing, though. That's probably very old stuff for him, Jon thought with an inaudible sigh.

Holly was looking very athletic and pretty when Tony suddenly dropped her rather roughly.

He grimaced, took a deep breath, and rubbed his shoulder.

"Are you all right?" Rhonda asked.

"Let's just go," he said.

They all climbed in, Holly and Rhonda in the rumble seat and Jon and Tony up front. Tony couldn't lift his captain out of a burning tank, Jon thought as he steered the roadster out onto Second Street. And a year later he can't lift little Holly into a car. Tony's wound wasn't even close to healed. Maybe he'd never be normal.

"I've never ridden in a rumble seat," Holly shouted over the exhaust noise as they drove downtown.

With the roadster's canvas top lowered, their heads and shoulders stuck up behind the windshield like four toy dolls in a little tin car. Two Snow Whites, Bashful and Grumpy, Jon thought with an amused shrug.

They crossed Division Street and drove up the hill to the Grand Theater. Jon pulled over to the curb and they read the theater posters from the street. *A Walk in the Sun*, starring Dana Andrews, was showing tonight.

Jon made a U-turn in the street and eased the front wheel of his roadster against the opposite curb. He left the engine idling, and jumped out. He ran up and read the small print on the poster under the marquee. It was a war movie. The ad promised stark realism.

I don't want to nurse Tony through another night, Jon thought. He ran back to the car.

"Let's not," he said.

They set out for Faribault, about fifteen miles south of Northfield.

Highway 3 had a dozen sharp ninety-degree corners that forced motorists to zigzag treacherously around rectangular farm fields. Jon took the corners fast enough to impress the girls. Their hair blew in the wind and they screamed.

Tony laughed out loud and took a long drink from his flask.

Near Faribault, Rhonda began to sing the ukelele songs "Five-Foot Two" and "Tonight You Belong to Me." Holly soon joined in.

Tony took several more slugs from his flask as the girls sang. On the final verse of the second song, Tony joined them, harmonizing with his resonant bass voice.

"You have a wonderful voice," Rhonda shouted over the engine and road noise. "Don't forget choir tryouts are on Monday."

Tony shrugged and took another drink.

Choir, Jon thought and frowned. Maybe he'd turn off Tony's alarm clock and let him sleep through the tryouts.

In Faribault, they watched Hitchcock's *Notorious*. Tony bought all four tickets. "You drove," he said to Jon.

Jon was only partly aware of the film's apparently excellent scenes, but he was very aware of Rhonda. Through some keen maneuvering, Jon ended up seated between Rhonda and Holly, with Tony on the other side of Holly—and Jon congratulated himself for it. At moments during the movie, Rhonda's arm touched Jon's and gave him incredible tingles. He longed to take her hand or put his arm around her. But he didn't dare. Not with the others there.

After the film, they wandered back to the roadster.

"I've never driven a car like this," Holly said.

"Do you know how to drive?" Jon asked.

"Hey, I drove in ice races back home," she said and grinned.

Holly took the wheel. Tony sat beside her in front and Jon and Rhonda slid down into the rumble seat.

Jon would've been much more aware of Rhonda's warm thigh against his, if not for Holly's insane and astonishing driving skills. She squealed away from the curb, the back tires chirping on the pavement as she speed shifted into second gear and then into third. She took the sharp corners on Highway 3 far faster than Jon had dared.

The tires screamed. Holly screamed.

"Faster," Tony shouted, taking another slug from his flask.

Holly obliged.

Holly screeched the roadster to a stop in front of the Northfield Bakery.

"That was fun," she said.

Jon marveled that they'd made it back at all.

"You can really drive," Tony said to Holly, his speech slightly slurred. "When did you learn?"

"When I was nine," she said. "My dad broke his leg and my mom worked. I was his chauffeur for six weeks. I could barely see over the dashboard."

"Well, you're hot behind the wheel," Tony said and whistled.

They all followed Rhonda into the bakery. First thing inside, Rhonda grabbed the telephone and called the police station.

"Elvira, this is Rhonda down at the Northfield Bakery. Tell Lenno I'll have a few friends in the front of the bakery until about one o'clock, okay?"

While Rhonda was on the phone, Tony ran back out to the car and grabbed the little paper bag from under the front seat. He stumbled slightly over the curb on his way back. He's losing it, Jon thought.

Rhonda hung up the phone and explained to the other three, "The police watch these main street shops all night. My sister's nervous about her reputation."

The light was subdued inside the bakery. The Clabber Girl clock on the wall above the cash register said eleven o'clock. Tony, Jon, and Holly sat at the counter. Rhonda stood behind it.

"Anyone who *doesn't* want one of my famous fountain Cokes—cherry? lemon?" Rhonda asked.

"Pretty soon we can have lemon Cokes in our room," Tony said. "We've got this tree and it has a little lemon on it."

"It's about this big." Jon made a walnut sized oval with his thumb and forefinger. "And it's green. It could be a lime, or an orange. It's probably through growing, though. The tree is dead."

"It's not dead—and it's a lemon."

"It's a dead orange," Jon shot back, laughing.

Tony laughed too and took a swipe at Jon's shoulder with his fist. He missed and nearly fell off his stool.

"You have a tree in your room?" Holly exclaimed.

"Yup. Someone threw it out on the street," Tony said. "We're nursing it back to health."

"Gee," Holly said. "Horticulturists."

Rhonda pointed at the chrome plungers on the soda fountain and asked, "So what'll it be?"

"Forget the lemon *and* the cherry," Tony said. "I've got something that will really perk up a Coke." He pulled a pint bottle out of the brown paper bag with a magician's flourish, as if he were pulling a rabbit out of a hat.

"What is it?" Holly asked.

"Sloe gin," Tony said. "Anyone ever had sloe gin and Coke?"

"Get that bottle off the counter," Rhonda ordered. "You're not underage, but the rest of us are. My sister would kill me if the police saw that bottle in here."

Tony slid the bottle off the counter and tucked it securely between his thighs.

"Holly and I are from Wisconsin," he said. "We were *weaned* on beer, weren't we?"

"Speak for yourself," Holly said.

"Four glasses, enchanting waitress," Tony said to Rhonda, "and no ice."

"Say please," Rhonda whispered, blinking her long eyelashes emphatically and smiling at Tony.

"Puh-lease."

Rhonda grinned and set the glasses on the counter.

Tony turned sideways so he couldn't be seen from the street. He carefully poured a half inch of gin into three of the glasses and an inch in the other.

"That one's mine," he said, making a little tink-tink on the glass with his fingernail, "since you kids are underage. Now a good dose of Coke syrup, a little ice, and fill 'em up with fizz, Rhonda, *puh-lease.*"

Jon had never heard Tony speak so easily, with so little inhibi-tion. Was it the girls? Jon wondered. Or the flask he'd been pull-ing at since seven o'clock?

"Yes, sir," Rhonda said, saluting. "Coming right up."

Tony tucked the bottle back between his legs. He crumpled the paper bag into a ball and with thumb and forefinger, aimed and threw it, dartlike, at Rhonda. It struck her in the back of the neck.

"Stop that," she said, laughing. She reached up and switched on the radio, tuning it to KDHL Faribault.

They all moved back to the same corner booth that Rhonda and Jon had sat in just a week earlier.

When the three of them were settled in the booth, Rhonda handed out the drinks. She gave Jon a funny smirk when she handed him his, then set the tray aside and sat down herself. With her first sip Rhonda said, "*Yum.* So, Tony. If you try out for choir you'll make it. I know you will. I'm not that confident about me, though. Too many sopranos are trying out."

"Don't worry," Jon said, "you'll do great."

"I'll worry until the recall list is posted next week."

"What's recall?" Tony asked.

"After tryouts," Jon said, glad to share what he had learned from his sister, "they post two lists—those who made it on the first try, and those who are recalled. My sister Trudy sometimes couldn't eat for three days waiting for those lists to appear."

"I know how she felt," Rhonda agreed. "I'm the same way."

"You'll make it, Rhonda, don't worry," Jon said, taking a long drink of the sloe gin Coke. He blinked in surprise and said, "Hey, this is good."

"Mine tastes kinda weak," Tony said. He reopened the pint bottle and poured more gin into his drink.

"Me too," Jon said, wanting to impress Rhonda.

"Are you sure?" Tony asked.

Jon nodded and took another swallow of the much stronger sloe gin Coke. It was the first alcoholic drink he had ever tasted that he liked. Not that he had tried much. A grand total of three drinks in his eighteen years and only mere sips from those, since he'd hated the tastes. Jon had never had much reason or opportunity to disobey his parents' strict rules about drinking.

The round of sloe gin Cokes disappeared completely.

"Want another one?" Tony asked.

"Sure," they all said at once and laughed.

Tony poured two really stiff ones—each filling nearly a third of the glass—and two weaker ones. He let the last of the gin drip out of the bottle, then laid the bottle down on the tray.

"Dead soldier," he muttered, sloppily making the sign of the cross over the prostrate bottle.

Rhonda stood up to carry the tray of glasses back to the soda fountain to fill them with cola. Jon noticed Tony catch her eye. With the faintest movement of his index finger and a tiny nod of his head, he motioned at the two glasses with triple shots. These are for us, his gesture said very plainly. A glimmer of a smile danced across Rhonda's lips as she turned away with the tray.

Jon burned at their conspiracy. He had to do something fast, or he'd lose her. She's *my* girl, he thought. No, he thought miserably, staring out the bakery window at the dark street. She's not my girl. Not yet. Loving someone doesn't make her your girl. Especially if you don't tell her.

Jon glanced at the clock. They only had a little more than a half hour before the girls had to get back.

Rhonda returned with the second round of sloe gin Cokes. "These are the two strong ones," she said, pointing to a couple of the glasses. Tony took one.

"I'll take the other," Jon said, looking to see if Rhonda was impressed. "You girls better eat a couple of peanut butter cookies before you go back to the dorm," Jon added, trying to sound knowledgeable and mature, "or you'll get campused for drinking."

"Oh," Holly said, "does that work?"

"Sometimes," Tony interrupted in a thick slur, "chewing peanuts will even fool a cop."

"No kidding," Rhonda exclaimed.

Jon was furious that Tony had upstaged him in his display of worldliness. Jon grabbed his drink and downed it in three big gulps.

"Let's dance," he said, jumping up and taking Rhonda's hand.

"Great idea," Rhonda said.

Holly walked over to the counter and turned up the volume on the radio, then walked back and took Tony's hand.

"Hey, baby," Tony said and stood up. He swung Holly around gracefully in spite of all he had drunk. Holly, with only a hint of concern in her eyes, laughed merrily.

After the ten o'clock news, KDHL Faribault always switched from oom-pa-pa polkas to slow dance music. The two pairs moved across the linoleum bakery floor, dancing to vocals by Barbara Whiting, Rosemary Clooney and Julius LaRosa.

"We're breaking all the rules tonight," Rhonda said and laughed. "Drinking, dancing."

"I've never broken any rules before," Holly replied. There was worry in her voice now.

"I'll bet you haven't," Tony drawled, pulling Holly close to his meaty chest. "You just stick with me. I'll teach you how much fun it is to break a few rules."

Over Rhonda's shoulder, Jon watched Tony and Holly dance. Tony was a very good dancer. He and Holly seemed to be floating across the bakery's linoleum floor. They began to spin, and spin. . . and spin. . .

Jon blinked slowly as he watched the bakery walls whirl around. He felt sensation leaving his legs. I should have eaten supper, he told himself.

Jon shook his head and the truth slowly penetrated his pulsating brain. Rhonda had given him Tony's stiff drink on the first round and Jon had made it even stronger. He had *chosen* a stiff one on the second round.

Jon couldn't feel his legs. But he most certainly felt a strong sensation between them. The beautiful and fluid movements he and Rhonda were making in so congested a space were beyond his comprehension. In a dreamlike voice that seemed to float into Jon's ears from a great and faraway distance, the announcer said over the radio, "Next you're going to hear the phenomenon whose honey voice has been banned in Boston: April Stevens singing Cole Porter's, 'I'm in Love Again'."

The song began. Jon's head swam. So did his body. Raw alcoholic courage surged through his veins. April Stevens' breathy, sensual voice stirred every sinew of romance and manhood in Jon's being. He pulled Rhonda in close and began to sing softly in her ear as they slowly danced. "I'm in love again. . . I'm in love again. . ."

They danced. Jon sang. Rhonda hummed. It was the most extraordinarily beautiful moment that Jon had ever experienced.

Then Jon said in a plaintive whisper, "I'm not in love *again*. I'm *still* in love."

Jon felt Rhonda's firm belly pressed against his hard and masculine response to the music, to the dance, and to Rhonda—his Scandinavian goddess, the sum total of everything feminine in the entire universe.

The pressure between his legs was becoming unbearable.

Jon slipped the open palm of his hand into the small of Rhonda's back, then slid it down even further, until his whole hand had gone uphill and then down again.

Suddenly, decisively, Jon pulled her hips hard into his erection and said, "Rhonda, I love you so much I can't stand it."

Then he passed out.

11

Jonathan Adamson skipped church.

He hadn't in years.

He had a head splitting hangover.

"Comin' over for lunch, Jon?" Tony asked just before noon.

"Nooooo," Jon said, groaning at the very idea of food.

"Want a 'hair of the dog'?" Tony held up his flask.

"Nooooo," Jon moaned. He rolled over slowly to escape the sight of Tony's ubiquitous flask.

"I'm going up the hall and get you some water," Tony said. "And I'm leaving some aspirin, right here on your desk. When I come back from the john you're going to take *all* the aspirin. And drink all the water, too, you hear? *All*."

Jon just groaned. And felt painfully stupid.

"Where's my car?" he rolled over and asked.

"Holly parked it on the street in front of your parents' house after she dropped us off."

"How did I get up here?"

"Flyboy and I carried you, and Boomer helped pull you up to your bunk."

About midafternoon, Jon managed to sit up. He still felt shaky, nauseated, and dizzy. Never again, he told himself.

He forced himself to get up, shower, and dress. He went to

supper believing he'd feel better if he ate something.

Jon entered the caf sheepishly, wishing he'd worn a sweat suit and a towel over his head so he could hide. He dreaded seeing Rhonda. I acted like a complete fool last night, he thought. And I passed out at her feet. What an idiot. Jon knew he'd have to apologize to Rhonda sooner or later. He hoped it would be later.

Jon shuffled toward the far corner of the caf in a cowering slump and slid his tray onto an empty table. He sat facing the wall, hoping Rhonda wouldn't recognize him from the rear.

He sipped coffee and nibbled at bread. Nothing else looked even slightly edible. The bread felt like concrete in his cotton mouth.

Suddenly Holly appeared at his elbow, pulled out a chair, and sat down beside him.

"You don't look so great," she said.

"I know. Thanks for driving last night."

"You mean home from Faribault?"

"I mean home from the bakery."

"I wouldn't have let either you or Tony drive." After a pause, she added, "That sloe gin is wicked stuff."

"I'm sorry I acted so stupid."

"You have nothing to be sorry for, Jon. I talked to Rhonda this morning. She feels pretty bad. She said you didn't know you were getting that first strong drink."

"Is Rhonda coming for supper?"

"She's practicing for tryouts. They're tomorrow. She's nervous as a blue jay. She and I have that much in common, anyway. I worry about everything."

"You do? You don't seem like the type."

"I hide it," Holly replied. She paused, then looked squarely at Jon and asked, "What do *you* hide?"

"I doubt you'd want to know," Jon said, attempting another tiny bite of bread.

"Sure I would," she smiled, taking a large gulp of milk.

"Well, okay. In junior high I used to hide being smart."

"You did that too? In my town in Wisconsin, being a 'brain' was like sudden death."

"It wasn't so bad for me after we moved to Northfield," Jon said, "but by then I was in ninth grade."

"In college it doesn't matter much."

"Being smart, you mean."

"It's not a sin, anyway," she said and smiled. "Speaking of sin, you and Rhonda were dancing pretty close last night."

"I know. I feel like a fool."

"You're not a fool," she said. She ate quietly for a minute, then leaned forward and said, "Jon, I need a favor."

For someone so accepting, so forgiving, Jon decided he'd do anything.

"Sure. What can I do?"

"A guy in my religion class asked me out for next Saturday. He's—I don't know how to say this—too nice to flat out refuse, but not nice enough to go out with."

"So what did you say?"

"I said I already had a date—and that's the favor. Could we do something on Saturday—so I wouldn't be lying?"

"I guess so. Sure," Jon said, "but this time I drive."

"No gin then."

They both laughed. After a pause Holly added quietly, "Or maybe you wanted to ask Rhonda for Saturday instead."

"I doubt she'll ever speak to me again after last night—much less go out with me. I have some serious apologizing to do."

"It was partly her fault," Holly said softly. "I told her so."

"I should have known better."

"Meanwhile, you're free to go out with someone like me, I guess, right? Someone more ordinary."

"Come on, Holly. Don't say that."

"It's true. Next to a 'chick' like Rhonda I look like a turkey."

"Now you're talking like Tony."

"He says that about me?"

"No. I mean he uses those words to describe girls."

"I'm glad you don't," Holly said. "You're a nice guy, Jon. One of the nicest I've met here. But I just don't want anyone to get hurt—not Rhonda, not you, and," she added with a tilt of her head and a small pretty smile, "especially not me."

"We'll just go out as friends then, okay?" Jon said. "No romance. Just friends."

"That will make it a whole lot easier," she said. "What time?"

"Let's decide tomorrow."

"Fine with me," she agreed. "Do I have to dress up?"

"Not at all."

Jon still felt queasy and headachy after his small supper, but he had to spend time in the library working on a history research paper. He edged into the library, hoping Rhonda wouldn't spot him. He didn't know yet how he could possibly apologize adequately.

The library closed at ten o'clock and Jon dragged himself downstairs to check his PO box before going to bed. He opened the tiny brass door and bent down to peek into the little cubicle.

Inside was a folded note. He recognized the handwriting instantly. Rhonda's. Jon's name in Rhonda's handwriting. Only a month earlier he would've treasured a note from her. But finding this note was more like a kick in the stomach than receiving a trophy. Jon feared reading her critical words about his pure stupidity. Ooh. Damn.

Jon didn't want to stand in the PO lobby and read her note. He didn't want anyone to see him gawk or rip his hair out. He tucked the note into his shirt pocket and trudged back through the leaves and the dark night to his room.

Tony was gone. Jon switched on his desk lamp, unfolded Rhonda's note, and smoothed out the single crease. The stark white note lay framed on Jon's forest green desk blotter pad. He glanced at the kneeling princess on his Land-O-Lakes crock, then bent over the note and read.

She started with just "Jon." Not "Dear Jon" or "Friend Jon" or

"My most beloved Jon." Ha. She'd never write "beloved" after last night, he thought.

It was just "Jon."

> Jon,
>
> Sorry for serving you that first—you know—Coke......... What if I had drunk it myself???????
>
> Guess what? Today at lunch Tony asked me out for next Saturday!!!!! I didn't think I should go, not yet, anyway. But I didn't want to say NO—not just like that. I mean, he fought our war for us, RIGHT??? So I fibbed and said you and I had talked about doing something together. Could we?? So I'd have an honest excuse???
>
> You'd better get rid of this note. I wouldn't want him to *find it* and get hurt.
>
> LET ME KNOW, OK ?????????????????????
>
> Rhonda

Jon grinned. He jumped up and drove his fist into the air. I'm forgiven, he thought, exhilarated. She actually apologized to *me* for giving me those drinks. And she wants me to go out with her.

Jon calmed down, sat on the edge of his desk, and kissed the note. Then he kissed the princess on the crock. He studied and restudied every word in Rhonda's note. There wasn't a shred of disgust in her tone at all.

"Get rid of this note," she had written. Ha. More likely he'd build an altar for it.

Strange, he thought. Both Holly and Rhonda want to use me for an excuse. Well, let them. This is *great*.

But what could he do? Suddenly an unnerving truth occurred to him: I have two dates for the same night.

Could the three of them do something together? Would Holly understand? Would Rhonda? Would Rhonda care that he'd already said yes to Holly? That worried Jon the most.

Jon stared at the princess on the crock. He needed a plan. He also had an even bigger problem. Tony was asking Rhonda out on dates. Somehow Jon had to put a stop to that.

Tony came in after midnight.

"You asleep, Jon?" he whispered.

"Not any more."

"You going out with Rhonda Saturday?"

"We're thinking about it." That wasn't a complete lie, at least.

"How about if I ask Holly and the four of us go together again?"

"Holly has a date," Jon said, assurance in his voice. At least that was the whole truth.

"Some other time, maybe," Tony said, sounding melancholy. He has such quick mood swings, thought Jon. Was it the drinking? Jon wondered what Tony had been like before the war.

Jon slid off his bunk and sat down on his desk chair. He looked straight at Tony and said firmly, "Maybe you shouldn't ask Rhonda out any more."

"Why not?"

"She's so young, for one thing."

"They're all young here," Tony said. "So what else am I supposed to do?"

"Just leave her alone, *okay?*"

"You mean leave her for you?"

"Something like that."

"That's a big order. She means that much to you?"

"Well, she's just Norwegian tail to you, right?"

Tony shrugged and rubbed his nose hard.

"This is important to me, Tony," Jon said quietly.

95

"Well, I'll do my best," Tony said finally. He walked across the room and slugged Jon gently on the shoulder.

"Promise?" Did I really say that?

"Promise."

Jon was surprised to see a breakfast line outside the caf the next morning. He tried to read a few paragraphs in his history book while he waited, then suddenly Rhonda ran up and squeezed in line beside him. The guy behind Jon scowled but she smiled sweetly at him and he melted.

"Hi, Jon. Did you get my note?" she asked.

Jon's heart pounded. He nodded.

"Rhonda," he blurted. "About last Saturday night. I'm really sor—"

Rhonda put her fingertip on Jon's lips. "You don't need to apologize. It was partly my fault."

Jon shook his head, wanting to take the blame.

"Everything you said and did was," she whispered so the others in line wouldn't hear, "the gin's doing. Besides, it was fun. So—what time are we leaving Saturday?"

This forgiveness felt like a transfusion to Jon. His headache disappeared, he straightened up, his mood soared. He was ready to say, "anytime." But then he remembered Holly. Ooh.

"Could we make it later?" he asked. "Say maybe nine o'clock, nine-thirty? I have to study for a test."

"Just come straight to the bakery," Rhonda said. "I'll look for you around nine."

Standing there in line, Jon longed to put his arms around her. His time would come. Saturday night for sure.

When they reached the entrance to the caf Rhonda said good-bye. "Wish me luck today, Jonathan," she added. "Choir tryouts are this afternoon."

"Aren't you going to eat?" Jon asked, looking puzzled.

"I have to practice," she said. She took one step back, patted the cheek of the guy who had scowled at her, then dashed off. The boy stood there, rubbing his cheek and wondering what hit him. Jon frowned and felt a stab of envy.

Later at lunchtime, Jon sat in the caf with Tony and a group of GIs.

"There's Holly," Tony said, nudging Jon's elbow. He shouted loudly across the cafeteria, "Hey, Holly. You're beautiful. Come eat with us."

Three football players at a neighboring table applauded. Holly arrived at the table blushing four hues of crimson. She sat down next to Jon.

Tony launched into a loud argument with Shark about the attractiveness of French women. Seeing that he was occupied, Holly leaned over and whispered in Jon's ear, "So what time should we meet on Saturday?"

Jon gulped. He didn't want Tony to hear that he had a date with Holly, too. The secret also had to be kept from Rhonda. This two date night, Jon thought, isn't going to be any cakewalk.

"Could we make it early?" Jon asked in a barely audible whisper. "I have to study for a test."

"How early?"

"Four-thirty? Five? Maybe go out for a burger, then take a drive? Try to get back by nine? That would be good—for my grade point average, I mean."

"That sounds like just what I need," Holly whispered and chuckled quietly. "A junior high date."

12

"Rhonda made it, first round," Holly announced excitedly as she slid her tray in next to Jon's, "and so did Tony."

Jon practically choked on his green beans. He knew exactly what Holly meant. They had both made choir. The *main* choir. The *big* choir.

"Good for them," was all Jon could manage to say.

"Look at them over there," Holly said, pointing. "That whole tableful got in on their first audition."

Jon glanced at the table. Tony saw him and waved. Tony pointed at himself and Rhonda and did a thumbs up. Jon waved, but without enthusiasm.

"Shark made it too?" Jon asked Holly.

"Which one is Shark?"

"The GI on Tony's right."

"He must have. Rhonda said that Dr. Christiansen was hungry for deep bass voices after the wartime shortages of men on campus."

Jon didn't see Tony again until almost eleven o'clock that evening. When Jon came in, Tony was at his desk studying and drinking. As usual.

"Congratulations," Jon said.

"About the choir you mean."

"Yes."

"Your beloved dark beauty got in too," Tony said, turning sideways in his chair.

"So I gathered from your celebration in the caf," Jon said. "You and Rhonda in the same choir makes me nervous."

Tony turned his back again and shrugged.

"You won't forget your promise?" Jon asked.

"No, sir, I sure won't," Tony said. He stood, snapped into a swift about-face, came to full attention, and saluted Jon. He looked ridiculous doing these maneuvers in his underwear. "It's firmly registered right up here," he said and tapped his temple with his saluting hand. "But you know, what might be harder is keeping my word to this Doc Christiansen guy, the leader of the choir."

"The director."

"Yeah. He asked me if I was willing to practice ten or twelve hours a week and give up my Easter break for a tour."

"And were you?"

"I said I was. But I can always quit."

"You won't quit. Nobody ever quits the St. Olaf Choir. Believe it or not, it's a huge honor around here to get into the main choir—especially for a freshman."

"Well," Tony said and snorted, "I don't know what the hell Holly and Rhonda have gotten me into."

Jon scarcely saw either Holly or Rhonda the rest of the week. On Saturday evening at four-thirty, Jon walked over to Mellby Hall to pick up Holly.

I have to bring this off, he told himself. My two date night will be the coup of the century.

He and Holly walked down St. Olaf Avenue and crossed over to Second Street to get the roadster.

"I heard that Tony asked Rhonda out," Holly said as they drove across the railroad tracks at the bottom of St. Olaf Avenue.

"I heard that too," Jon said. "I also heard she begged off."

"He's so, I don't know, so *masculine*," Holly said.

"What does that make me?" Jon asked, glancing over at her as he pulled up for a stop sign.

"Darn you, Jon, you know *exactly* what I mean."

"You mean you're safe with me," Jon said.

"I suppose so," Holly said with a cute smirk. "We're the same that way."

"Inexperienced," Jon said.

"Right."

"Guys do the same with that," Jon said, "as some kids do with being smart. We hide it."

"It's nice that girls don't have to hide something like that. Besides, it'd be pretty hard for me to pretend that I was experienced when I'm not," Holly said with a chuckle.

"I know how that goes. Tony figured me out right away."

"Innocence isn't something to be ashamed of," Holly said.

"Maybe not, but I'd at least like to be a *little* scary."

Holly laughed. Jon liked her laugh. It was warm and deep. He felt strange talking this way with a girl. They were discussing sex—without even using the word.

"So where are we going?" Holly asked.

Jon steered the roadster past Laird Stadium on the north edge of the Carleton campus, then east on Highway 19 and out of town.

"I thought we could go to Cannon Falls and see what movie's showing over there," Jon suggested.

"If the movie's terrible," Holly said, "we could find a booth somewhere in Cannon Falls and talk."

"Good idea," Jon agreed. They drove a few minutes in silence, then Jon said, "You know, it seems like I've spent my whole life driving to some other town looking for excitement."

"It was the same in Forest Mills."

"That's your town? Forest Mills? Where's Forest Mills?"

"In the middle of Great Wisconsin Nowhere—unless you work in a lumbermill or ski. Then you might know where Forest Mills is. It's near Hayward about ten miles north of the Telemark ski area."

"I've heard of Telemark. Before the war, ski buses went there from St. Olaf every weekend in the winter. St. Olaf kids ski there all the time."

"I know. The first date of my life was at Telemark—two years ago. With a Norwegian exchange student from St. Olaf. He got stuck here in Minnesota and couldn't go home when the Nazis took over Norway. He was twenty-two and I was fifteen."

"How did that go—you being with a guy that old?"

"It didn't work. He was slow on skis but way too fast with his hands. On the hill I could keep out of his reach most of the time."

Jon laughed, picturing that pursuit on the slopes.

"Now that the war is over," Holly went on, "I wonder if St. Olaf will send buses again."

"Maybe so. A lot of things are getting back to normal finally."

"I read in a ski magazine that they're opening Sun Valley again," Holly said. "It was a navy rehabilitation center for most of the war."

"Have you skied there?" Jon asked.

"When I was about ten. My dad took a youth group and I went along."

"Is he a teacher, or what?"

"A pastor."

"You're a P-K. A skiing preacher's kid."

"I was born a P-K, and born with skis on, too," Holly said, and chuckled.

"How did your mother enjoy that?"

"You know, I've said that a hundred times," she said, kicking Jon's ankle gently, "but I've never pictured it before. Do you ski?"

"I just started last year. I've skated all my life though. That seems to make skiing easier. *I* was born with *skates* on."

"Instant episiotomy."

"What's that?"

"Nothing. A word I learned at the Hayward hospital. I was a nurse's aide."

Jon realized he felt really relaxed with Holly. But he kept glancing at his watch. He began to count down the minutes to nine o'clock and his rendezvous with Rhonda. With a bit of guilt.

Jon and Holly cruised into Cannon Falls. *The Bells of St. Mary's* was playing at the Cannon Theater. They had both seen it before. Bing Crosby starred as a singing priest and Ingrid Bergman played one of the nuns.

"I laugh when I think of her as a nun," Holly said, shaking her head at Bergman's picture posted on the Cannon Theater's big marquee.

Holly and Jon decided to talk instead of seeing the movie a second time. They sat in a cafe for more than an hour, munching onion rings and slurping malts. At seven-thirty they drove down to the park by the falls. They walked along the weedy bank, throwing pebbles into the river. The water slipped over the dam by the power plant in soothing laps.

Jon enjoyed talking with Holly. He liked that about her—that they could just talk. He asked more questions about her parents and learned that they'd both gone to Luther College in Iowa.

"They're just as glad I'm going to St. Olaf," Holly said, biting at a loose thread on her blouse sleeve. "It's closer."

"Here," Jon said. He fished his penknife out of his pocket and cut the thread for her.

At eight o'clock Jon began to worry about getting back. He considered pretending to fall into the river, to use that as an excuse for returning early. But then he thought about how long it would take to change clothes.

Holly caught him sneaking a look at his watch.

"Are you bored?" she asked quietly.

"No," Jon said. "No. I've had a great time."

"We should go back, though, if you're going to have enough time to study for your test."

Jon nodded and they headed back to the car. Within fifteen minutes they were sitting in the roadster outside Agnes Mellby Hall. Because he was running late, Jon had decided to risk taking his car on campus. He didn't want to keep Rhonda waiting.

"I enjoyed myself tonight," Holly said, "or should I say this afternoon." She grinned. He tried.

"So did I," Jon replied, chuckling. "Good thing we agreed it wasn't going to be romantic." He smiled at her.

Holly looked away and didn't respond.

They sat in silence for a minute, then Holly turned sideways in her seat and looked Jon directly in the eye.

"I like you, Jon," she said. "I like you a lot. If you ever get Rhonda out of your brain, let me know, okay?" She put the palms of her hands on his cheeks and kissed him quickly on the lips. Then she jumped out of the roadster and ran toward her dorm.

Wide-eyed and surprised, Jon felt his lips with his fingertip. He mused on Holly's kiss for half a minute, then slammed the roadster into gear, and roared out of the parking lot. He was late for his date with Rhonda.

He sped downtown and parked behind the bakery. His watch said nine-twenty. Late. He worried that Rhonda would be upset, and maybe not even be there.

Suddenly Rhonda swung open the bakery's back door and called, "Hello, Jonathan. Come on in."

Jon gawked. She was wearing a bathrobe and slippers.

"Pardon my getup," she said and grinned. "I'm spending the night. My clothes were covered with flour so I changed into my robe. I hope you don't mind."

Did he *mind?* Jon smiled and shook his head.

"Let's go right up front," she said. Then she locked the door behind them.

They sat down, once again in the corner booth and across from each other. I'm in heaven, he thought.

"So, tell me about Tony," Rhonda said.

Suddenly exasperated and deflated at this unwelcome request, Jon scratched his cheek for a second and glanced toward the soda fountain. He wondered how to steer the conversation away from her favorite subject of the moment. Jon glanced back at Rhonda and nearly gasped. She had leaned forward and her robe had poofed open. Jon had an aerial view of both her breasts, which rested like inverted melon halves on the booth top. He didn't dare look straight at them, but he saw plenty with every furtive glance.

Wanting to keep her right where she was, Jon quickly launched into a whole series of Tony stories. As he jabbered away, Rhonda looked into his eyes at times, and at other moments nodded and stared out the window. Those were Jon's stolen viewing sessions.

He told about Tony's war wounds, his drinking sprees, his nightmares, his beloved lemon tree—fully a dozen Tony stories.

She listened. He talked. She looked off into space. He stared.

Jon had never seen bare breasts. This unique opportunity probably would have caused him to faint had it not been for the uncomfortable congestion between his legs.

When he finally finished his soliloquy, Rhonda leaned back and said, "Tony has had a pretty rough time of it."

"I guess so. A lot of them have. It will take awhile for them to get back to normal."

"Whatever that is," Rhonda quickly added. "What is normal, Jonathan? Are you normal? Am I?"

"Who knows?" Jon replied with a shrug. He was beginning to calm down, now that her robe again covered her dark nipples. Whew. "Anyway—that's enough about Tony," he said. "Tell me about you."

"What do you want to know?"

"Everything. You once wrote on my *Wizard of Oz* program, 'Next stop, Hollywood.' Were you serious?"

"Yes," she said intently. "I want to sing in musicals. The St. Olaf Choir is my first stop."

"Well, you got in—and you're certainly pretty enough." He attempted the first line of "You Oughta Be in Pictures."

"Oh, Jon," Rhonda said, laughing warmly and leaning forward to pat his cheek. She exposed her breasts again. Yikes. Jon's heart did a triple flip. "Do you remember what you said to me when we were dancing last week?"

"Are you kidding? Of course I remember."

"You can take it back if you want," she said—and then added with a big smile, "now that you're sober."

Just then, Rhonda's sister marched downstairs, also in robe and slippers, and with a towel wrapped around her hair.

"Look, Rhonda," she said. "We weren't too pleased about your party last Saturday night, and now you're down here running around with next to nothing on."

"Oh, come on, Sis," Rhonda said, pointing to Jon. "This is Jonathan Adamson. You've met his mother. He's okay."

"Everybody you bring here is *okay*," her sister said, her words heavy with sarcasm.

"Look," Jon said, standing up. "I was just going anyway."

"You don't have to," Rhonda said firmly.

"Yes, he does," her sister said, turning and shutting the upstairs door behind her.

Jon followed Rhonda back through the workroom. "I sure don't want to cause any trouble," he insisted.

"Never mind. She's always been that way. She thinks she's my mother."

Rhonda unlocked the back door and swung it open. They stood in the dim light of the parking lot.

"You're afraid of me, aren't you?" she asked.

"I suppose I am, a little."

"Because I'm a year older than you are?"

"Nah," Jon said, denying it, but knowing that age and maturity were a big part of it. She had been around, for sure.

"Well, Jonathan," Rhonda said, leaning close to him, "I want you to know that you're one of the nicest looking guys I've ever seen." Her face was just inches from his.

He tilted his head and moved his lips toward hers.

"Rhonda," her sister barked from an upstairs window. "*Now.*"

Jon jerked back.

"Bye, Jonathan," Rhonda whispered. She nodded over her

shoulder in the direction of the upstairs window. "Sorry about her. She is so darn strict."

Rhonda ran back into the bakery and closed the door behind her. It was over.

Jon turned and tried to walk normally toward his car. The pressure in his jeans made the trip difficult.

Seated in the roadster, Jon adjusted his jeans and started the engine. The Model A was far noisier than it should have been at that delicate moment.

Tony was right about the Model A, Jon thought. It wasn't designed for romance.

13

Jon hadn't counted on so much romance during his first semester in college. He'd decided the previous summer not to do anything extra in his first year on campus—not debate, not theater, not sports. He wanted to spend his time studying.

But he hadn't counted on romance. Many evenings after his two date night, he tried hard to study, but too often all he could think of was Rhonda—with some strangely mixed warm and guilty feelings about Holly thrown in.

Now that choir was rehearsing, Tony and Rhonda ate meals together in the caf every couple of days, though usually they weren't alone. Jon supposed the others who sat with them were also choir members. Sometimes Tony or Rhonda called Jon over and he'd go eat with them. But he usually felt as if he was horning in on them.

One day in mid-October, Jon saw Tony and Rhonda eating supper together, just the two of them. Jon caught Tony's eye from across the caf and raised his eyebrows.

"Look, Jon," Tony said later in the library lobby, "she invited me over to her table. What could I do?"

"You promised."

"Okay," Tony said with a slight sneer. "Next time she asks me I'll say this, 'I can't eat with you because you've turned my room-mate into a frickin' moon faced love zombie.' That okay?" he asked, his voice dripping with irony.

"Don't you break your word," Jon ordered, then stormed away.

The communication remained strained for a few days, then gradually cooled. Both Jon and Tony were suddenly too preoccupied with demanding reseach papers and the grind of daily studying to give much thought to promises either kept or broken.

After a week, Jon and Tony had calmed down and were back to their normal controlled relationship. The days grew shorter, the studying more intense, and the campus—having for weeks been at its most beautiful in autumn reds and yellows and golds—now seemed more open and expansive with the leaves off the trees.

At dawn on a Thursday morning, Tony shook Jon awake. "Boo!" he yelled in Jon's ear. "Get up, Peckerhead. It's Halloween!"

Jon yawned and dressed, grateful that Tony was in a good mood instead of one of his too common foul tempers.

Jon buttoned his shirt and watched Tony fuss with the tree, thumbnailing off a few withered leaves.

"This thing has some new buds," Tony exclaimed. "Look."

Jon bent over the tree.

"What do you know," he said. "Beats me how buds can grow on a dead tree."

"Dead trees," Tony said, with a slug to Jon's stomach, "do not grow leaves or lemons."

"Oranges," Jon said and smirked.

Jon studied the tiny green citrus fruit suspended from the tree's top branch. It had grown another fraction of an inch in the past few days, he noticed.

"Maybe now that the heat is finally on in here," Tony added, pointing at the radiator, "this little tree thinks it's spring and is really on a growth spurt."

"Only it's Halloween," Jon said, looking out at the golden leaves on the lawn.

Tony turned to the mirror and attempted to yank a comb through his unruly curls. "So," he asked, "is Halloween a national holiday in Northfield?"

"No. But we have fun. Last year we opened fire hydrants all over town with a pipe wrench and played scoop shovel."

"What the hell is scoop shovel?"

"You tie a long rope on a shovel then put it in the road like it fell out of someone's pickup truck. When somebody stops and jumps out to pick it up, you pull it away with the rope and run."

"Ooooh. That sounds downright risqué."

"Well, we thought it was fun."

At breakfast, Tony and Jon joined a tableful of Tony's GI friends. He hoped Rhonda would see him with those older men.

"You hear about Greasemonkey?" Flyboy asked no one in particular, his face bent over his cereal bowl. "He got kicked out of school—for good."

Everybody shrugged.

"So that's why I haven't seen him around," Boomer said.

"Did your daddy tell you what happened to Greasemonkey?" Shark asked Jon.

"He never tells me anything," Jon said. "But I heard from a guy in my English class. Greasemonkey got caught with a girl in his room, right?"

"Yup."

"Gloria Tanager?" Shark asked.

"Gloria's sitting right over there," Tony said, pointing. "If it had been her, she'd have been kicked out too."

"That's a big risk," Jon said, "a girl in your room."

"A lot of the GIs are doing it," Flyboy said. "I mean, where else can you take a girl in this town?"

Nobody said anything to that.

"Any of you idiots remember it's Halloween?" Tony asked.

Shark looked at his Swiss calendar watch. "Yup. Appears to be the thirty-first," he said.

"Let's have a party," Tony said. "A big party with buckets of beer. I heard there were caves near the campus somewhere."

"The sandstone caves," Jon offered. The local authority.

"Are they far from here?"

"At Heath Creek, just over the backside of the hill. Less than a mile."

"An easy walk for a foot soldier," Boomer said. "How you birdmen gonna get there?"

"I suppose you'll flap your wings over the trees," Shark said, giggling and nudging Flyboy.

"Shut up, you nitwits," Tony said. "Jon, let me borrow your car this afternoon. I'll go to Dundas and get us some high point beer."

"You can't take his putt-putt to buy beer, asshole," Flyboy said, shaking his head at Tony. "He's the dean's kid."

Tony shrugged. "So let me borrow your car," he said.

Flyboy snorted, and replied, "Nobody drives my iron but me. I'll drive you to Dundas."

"Good," said Tony. "I'll buy the beer. But we better not get caught. Buying beer for babies could get us kicked out of school."

"I could use a vacation," Flyboy said, "but nobody's going to get caught."

"The police drive by those caves every night," Jon warned.

"They'll be too busy in town," Tony said, "chasing kids playing scoop shovel."

"How do you know about scoop shovel?" Flyboy asked.

Tony pointed at Jon.

"Dumb city kid," Flyboy said to Jon, nodding at Tony. "Never heard of scoop shovel."

"Go over and invite Gloria Tanager," Tony said to Flyboy. "She can do a vampire dance to liven up the party."

"Sure, why not," Flyboy said. He jumped up and strutted over to Gloria's table.

Just then Rhonda and Holly appeared with their trays and sat down at the next table.

"Happy Halloween," Rhonda called over her shoulder to Jon. "Is anybody planning a party?"

"How about letting those two girls come too?" Tony said to the group of GIs, gesturing over his shoulder with his thumb.

Everybody shrugged.

"Party in the caves tonight. You're invited," Tony said to Rhonda and Holly.

"Just the two of us?" Holly asked. "With all of you? Ha."

"Gloria Tanager's coming," Flyboy added with a broad smile.

"That will make Holly feel perfectly secure," Rhonda said and giggled.

"We'll invite some others your age," Shark said, "won't we, Tony?"

Tony nodded.

Everybody waited for Holly and Rhonda's response.

"I don't know," Holly whispered. Jon just barely heard her.

"It's a Thursday," he heard Rhonda whisper back. "We have to be in by ten forty-five. What could possibly happen?"

"Plenty."

"Well, if it gets crazy we can leave."

Holly shrugged.

"Settled," Tony said, smiling and nudging Jon.

Late that afternoon, Jon helped Tony carry a load of party supplies to Flyboy's car. With Flyboy at the wheel of his maroon pre-war Plymouth, the three of them drove to within one hundred yards of the caves.

Jon pointed and said, "That cave would be best for a party. I've been inside it before. It's like a round room and even has a table."

Jon lugged a cardboard box full of candles, pretzels, chips, and bottled pop from the car to the cave entrance. Tony and Flyboy followed behind, each carrying a case of beer.

Two greasy kids who looked like they were posing for a Wildroot Cream Oil ad were crouched at the mouth of the cave smoking cigarettes. They smirked at Jon and stayed crouched in the sandy gravel.

"Beat it," Tony barked.

The kids jumped up. They shot Tony a defiant look but quickly slunk away.

Inside the cave, Jon showed them the table—a huge cable spool someone had rolled down from the highway. On the sandstone walls were dozens of chinks carved throughout the years as candleholders. Hundreds of candles had burned in those chinks over the decades. Dripped wax of every color decorated the walls.

Jon grabbed the candles out of the box and placed them around the cave. Tony struck a match and lit them all. "This'll be great tonight," he said. "Spooky as hell."

"Yeah," Jon and Flyboy agreed.

Jon picked up Holly and Rhonda at seven o'clock. They headed down the southwest hill from Manitou Heights, across Highway 19, and over the slope to Heath Creek.

"What's the cave like?" Holly asked Jon.

"Just a big old cave, high and round. They say Jesse James hid in it after the bank raid. I don't think so, though. History always gets twisted over the years."

"That's your major, isn't it?" Holly asked.

"Is it really, Jon?" Rhonda said. "I didn't know that. Are you going to be a teacher or what?"

"I'm going to be a big Hollywood film producer—historical epics and musicals—all box-office hits. Maybe a remake of *The Wizard of Oz*," Jon said and grinned at Rhonda.

She grinned back.

The air was steamy inside the cave, the party well under way when the three of them arrived. They dropped their coats on top of a pile of other coats on the floor. Flyboy was playing bartender, which meant opening bottles of pop and beer and pointing to the pretzels and chips.

"Want a beer?" he asked Rhonda.

"Sure," she said. "How about you, Holly?"

"I've never tried beer."

"Now's your chance," Rhonda said.

Jon took a Dr. Pepper. "I've learned my lesson," he whispered to Holly.

Holly tasted her beer and stuck out her tongue, repulsed. She handed her bottle to Tony and went back to Flyboy for a Coke.

Most of the girls had come dressed as witches. Gloria Tanager was a black cat. She wore black tights, a low-cut black blouse, and a black hat. A cat mask with whiskers covered her nose and eyes and cheekbones. That feline creature is scary in almost every way, thought Jon.

Jon wore the red devil costume he'd worn in a church play a couple of years earlier, red long underwear—now too tight—with a long tail sewn on at the rear.

Gloria suddenly spotted Jon and screamed. "Oh, I just can't resist the devil!" she cried. She grabbed Jon's tail and pulled him close to her. She wrapped her arms tightly around his waist and said, her lips nearly touching his, "Well, aren't you a cute little blond Norwegian boy."

Her breath smelled of beer and cigarette smoke. Her hair smelled like lavender.

Jon felt dizzy and his ears began to ring.

"Are you nuts?" Flyboy called to Gloria from his post at the bar. "That's the dean's kid. They'll lock you up."

Gloria pushed herself away from Jon and pounced feline style, claws poised, across the cave. She fell into Flyboy's arms. "You *are* cute," she called to Jon, blowing him a kiss.

Jon turned away and took a big gulp of Dr. Pepper to revive himself. He wandered around the candlelit cave for a few minutes, studying the party scene.

Most of the guys had made only half-hearted tries at costumes—Frankenstein stitches penned on their cheeks, front teeth covered with Blackjack gum.

Except for Flyboy and Gloria, no one really paired off with anyone. That was okay with Jon, since Holly and Rhonda were both there.

Jon wasn't keeping track, exactly, but it seemed that the GIs were drinking most of the beer. Gloria was easily keeping up with them too. Within a half hour the place got really noisy.

Boomer suddenly turned to Gloria and shouted, "Show us how the witch's black cat dances, Gloria baby."

"Yeah," the GIs shouted.

The gallon of beer that Gloria had poured into her ample black cat body made her more than up to it.

Shark and Boomer dropped pebbles into empty beer bottles and began to shake them at a slow steady beat. Flyboy picked up the rhythm, patting his thighs with the palms of his hands. Boomer started to hum the striptease song, "Dum dum dum, ta dum dum dum. . ." Jon envisioned GIs in war-torn towns all over the world, in bars, in pubs, in the streets, creating diversion from their nightmares.

Gloria thrived on the attention. In the dim candlelight, she stepped up on the cable spool. Everyone formed a circle around her and she began to dance earnestly, responding to the makeshift music as seriously as if it were being played by Stan Kenton or Gene Krupa.

Gloria began to rub her body, slowly, sensually, with both of her hands. Starting at her knees, she slid her palms over the insides of her thighs, moved her fingers around and across her hips. Then she cupped her breasts in her hands, her body thrusting hard to the beat.

Some of the younger girls looked embarrassed. Their hands over their eyes, they giggled and ooohed quietly and peeked between their fingers.

Holly moved next to Jon and whispered, "I shouldn't have come here. I'm leaving."

"You can't walk back alone," he said.

"I don't care. I can't stay here."

They slipped out together.

At the cave's entrance, Jon glanced back at the party. Gloria had pulled the top of her blouse down around her hips. She ran her fingers over her lacy black brassiere.

"Holy smoke," Jon said to Holly. "Look."

Holly turned for a second. "Oh boy," she said.

She walked up the grassy hillside with determination. "My dad was so happy I decided to go to a nice, safe Lutheran college," she said with a sigh.

Holly stopped suddenly. "What about Rhonda?" she asked.

"You're right. Wait here. I'll go back and get her."

Jon ran back down the hill and into the cave.

"Holly and I are leaving," he whispered to Rhonda. "You'd better come with us."

"I'm having fun," she said, taking another sip of beer.

"I'll walk Holly to the dorm and then come back for you, okay?"

"Sure," Rhonda said. "Thanks."

Back outside the cave in the cold night air, Jon told Holly, "She wants to stay."

"She shouldn't," Holly retorted.

"I said I'd go back for her."

"Why don't you just stay too," Holly said in an expressionless voice. "I can make it by myself. The moon's so bright you can practically see the dorm from here."

"I'll walk you to the top of the hill, anyway," Jon said.

They trudged silently up the back road to the campus. At the top of the hill Holly said, "I'll be fine now. You can go back and rescue Rhonda from that pack of wild animals."

"That *was* pretty wild," Jon agreed.

"Sure was," Holly said. She turned away and began walking toward her dorm. "Goodnight, Jon," she called over her shoulder. "Thanks for being my escort."

"You're welcome," Jon called back.

He stood there a minute and watched Holly disappear around the corner of Mellby Hall. He was suddenly aware of his devil costume and how silly he looked. He didn't want to look stupid when he walked Rhonda back to her dorm, so he sprinted across campus to Ytterboe, his tail in hand. Back in his room, he quickly wiggled out of his costume, dressed in jeans, then ran back over the brink of the hill and toward the caves.

The valley seemed surprisingly quiet. Were they telling ghost stories? Jon wondered.

He peeked in the cave's entrance, then stepped inside. Except for a few flickering candles, empty bottles, and cardboard boxes, the place was deserted.

He puzzled over the empty cave all the way back to campus. Had someone been hurt? Was the party raided? Whatever it was it happened quickly. He'd only been gone about twenty minutes.

Back in his dorm room, Jon plopped down on his desk chair and found himself thinking about Gloria. Was she nursing those GIs' war wounds? he wondered. Jon had so many questions about the whole process—men and women wrapped together, pushed together, caressing each other, much like Gloria had caressed herself tonight. Jon wondered when he'd ever be ready for that.

Rhonda would be there for that moment, he thought. He'd make sure of it. Making love to Rhonda would be beyond ecstasy. Though of course his mother would expect them to be married first. Of course.

Tony stumbled into the room after midnight. Jon reached under his mattress and pulled out his flashlight. He snapped it on so Tony wouldn't trip. Tony pulled a handful of candles out of his jacket pocket and laid them on his desk.

"It's lucky you and Holly left when you did," he said, his speech in its usual post-midnight slur. "We were raided. The cops came."

"I bet those two high school kids you kicked out of the cave squealed on us," Jon said.

"Maybe. Anyhow, they got us for trespassing and for underage possession."

"What about Gloria?" Jon asked.

"Indecent exposure. She was down to not much when the cops came in. And they kept asking who bought the beer."

"Uh-oh-" Jon said.

"No one squealed, thank God," Tony said. "I can't afford to get kicked out of school."

After a pause, Jon asked, "And what about Rhonda?"

"I walked her back to Mellby."

"You walked her back—and that's all?"

"Cross my heart. I'm innocent as hell," Tony said, taking a swig from his flask.

"Hell is not," Jon replied, yanking his blanket up to his chin, "the home of the innocent."

14

"Did you get one?" Tony asked the next morning. They often crossed paths on the sidewalk on their way to their 10:50 classes.

"One what?" Jon asked.

"A summons from the DEAN, you know, your daddy. Seems everybody at the party got one."

"I'll check my PO."

Sure enough, a note from his father was waiting for Jon in his post office box.

November 1, 1946

THE CAVE MEN
Jonathan Adamson '50
St. Olaf College

Dear Jonathan,

The Northfield Police Department has given me your name as one of our students attending a drinking party in the Heath Creek caves. I am calling together all of the men involved at 4 PM Monday, November 4, in my office. Please be there promptly.

C. R. Adamson
Dean of Men

There was a note added in his father's handwriting.

Jon: Could you stop in beforehand, say about three o'clock, and talk to me ? Thanks.

CRA.

Jon stood in the lobby and read the summons again. The Cave Men, he thought. Pretty funny. His dad did have style.

Back in September, Jon had heard that a navy GI, one of the "Canoe Crew" as Tony called them, had nightmares and kept falling out of his upper bunk in Ytterboe. Jon's dad had told the GI, "You better lay low for awhile."

Jon waited outside his father's office at three o'clock on Monday. He tried to prepare himself for the meeting by whispering the DEAN several times in a facsimile of Tony's deep sarcastic voice. He tried squeaking "the freshman" also, but in the smallest voice he could audibly muster. Jonathan Adamson knew his place, and it was definitely subordinant to his father.

His father had always felt responsible for Jon's behavior, Jon knew that, but only as a father, never before as Dean Adamson dealing with a St. Olaf freshman named Jonathan Adamson.

Jon knew his father well enough not to worry that he'd lecture or be unfair, but he did think his father might be disappointed. Jon hadn't disappointed his father very often. Thinking back to the times he had, he remembered not liking the feeling at all.

"You can go in now, Jon," the secretary said. Jon had seen her dozens of times, both in the office and at their house. She was perpetually smiling—but today she gave him a different kind of smile—an understanding, knowing, sympathetic, almost conspiratorial one.

"Thanks," he said, without enthusiasm.

"Come in, Jon," his father said, "and sit down. I'll be right with you." He scribbled his signature at the bottom of several typed letters lying on his desk, then pushed them aside. He raised his head and released a resigned, let's get this over with sigh. "Tell me about the cave party."

"What do you want to know?"

"How it started. Your part in it. Who bought the beer."

"To begin with," Jon said, "I told them where the caves were. And I helped carry stuff down before the party."

"That's a start," his father said and nodded. "Tell me more."

"The guys just wanted to get together in a spooky place for Halloween. I didn't think it would do any harm."

"You knew there'd be drinking, didn't you?"

"Sure. But the guys brought pop for those who didn't want to drink beer. I couldn't see any harm in it."

"It's against the rules."

"We were off campus. I thought it would be okay."

"It would have been okay, as you put it, if everyone there had been over twenty-one, which they weren't, and if you had gotten permission to be on that private property, which you hadn't."

"No one ever asks permission to use those caves," Jon insisted. "I thought you told me *you* used them back when *you* were a student—right?"

"I guess you have me there," his father said and chuckled. He paused, then asked seriously, "Who bought the beer?"

"I can't tell you," Jon said.

"Can't or won't?"

"I guess it's won't."

"Loyalty is a good trait—but it sometimes has serious consequences—like now."

"You didn't raise me to be a squealer."

"I guess not," he said and sighed. "Well, Jon, I also called you in early to warn you that I'll have to treat you just like all the others who were caught in the raid."

"I know that," Jon replied. "I wouldn't expect anything else from you."

"The judicial board has left it up to me. Paulsrud, the one who always wears a flight jacket. . ."

"They call him Flyboy," Jon broke in.

"Flyboy, then. The police will probably charge Flyboy with supplying alcohol to minors, since his car was there."

"But he. . . ," Jon started to say, then caught himself.

"But he what?"

"I meant," Jon said, "uh, what will you do to him?"

"I can't discuss that with you. I expect he'll have a brief and unscheduled vacation from school," his father replied. He took a deep breath and went on. "You're sure you don't want to tell me any more?"

"Positive."

"Very well."

There was a pause. Then Jon said, "You know I left early, don't you?"

"What do you mean?"

"I left early from the party. Holly Hanson and I. We weren't even there when the police came."

"How did your name get on the list then?"

Jon thought about that for a few seconds, then it dawned on him. "Those two high school jerks must've reported me," he said. "They saw me there that afternoon."

"If you really weren't there at the time of the raid, one of the policemen will remember. Then you shouldn't be liable. I could call the station. They know you."

"You don't need to do that," Jon said.

"Do you want to come in with the others or not?" his father asked, obviously trying to be fair.

"I guess I should come in. I helped set up the party and everyone knows it. And I was there. Some of them might not even know I left early. If you let me off, it'll look like a fix."

"Thanks," his father said. They both knew it would make his

job easier.

"I'll come back with the others at four o'clock," Jon said.

"One more thing," his father added as Jon stood up to leave. "We have hundreds of veterans on campus this year. Most of them obey the rules like Boy Scouts."

"I know that."

"Don't let that small group of tough GIs—Tony and his buddies—pull you into anything else."

"I won't," Jon said, not at all sure what he was agreeing to.

"I can find you another room any time you say."

"I want to make it work if I can," Jon replied.

"Be careful."

"I will."

"That wasn't so bad," Tony said as they left Jon's father's office at four-thirty. "Two weeks probation. I can handle that."

"What did you think of his speech?" Jon asked.

"It made sense. He's right," Tony said. "This joint isn't going to change very fast."

"Like the dean said, it'll be a few years," Flyboy added with a laugh, "before they start serving beer in the cafeteria."

As the two of them waved goodbye to Flyboy and stepped into their room, Jon asked Tony, "If you were president of St. Olaf, what would *you* change?"

"I don't know," Tony said, rubbing his chin. "Everybody's so Norweeeeegian here."

"We can't help that."

Tony dropped his books on his desk top, then glanced at his watch. "Speaking of Norweeeeegians," he said, "let's go find Rhonda and Holly at the caf and see what Dean Hillstrom did to the cave women."

"Okay."

"And Jon. Thanks for not ratting on me."

"I told you the first day of school that I'd never squeal."

"I can't afford to get kicked out. St. Olaf is important to me.

Thanks. No more cave parties."

"Flyboy's the one you should thank," Jon said. "He's taking the rap. A whole week's suspension."

"Well, it seemed like he *wanted* to, the crazy bastard," Tony said. "He sits there smiling at your daddy, saying that a week off in corn picking season is perfect timing for an Iowa farm boy. A true lunatic. But I'll pay his fine."

"Yeah. Dad sure looked surprised at Flyboy's response," Jon said. "But Flyboy really seemed to want a week off. Maybe the academic pressure's getting to him."

"It's getting to me, too," Tony said, grabbing his books again and leading the way across the brown, November campus to supper.

"Dean Hillstrom has spies," Rhonda told Tony and Jon as they ate. "I'm sure of it."

"Don't look at me," Holly said, her hands held high in innocent surrender. "I don't even *know* everything that Gloria did."

"She did plenty, and she's out for a whole semester," Rhonda reported, shaking her head and frowning.

"That'll be good for Flyboy," Tony said. "He can get her out of his system."

"What did Dean Hillstrom do to the rest of you?" Jon asked Rhonda.

"We're campused for a month. All of us. Except for Holly here who happened to have left before the raid," Rhonda said, a touch of bitterness in her voice.

"You have no idea how lucky I am that I wasn't caught," Holly said. "If my father had found out, I'd have been suspended forever."

"He wouldn't do that," Jon asked, "would he?"

"He might. He's pretty strict. He has to be."

"In that case, I count myself the lucky one," Rhonda said, tossing her hair over her shoulder emphatically.

Jon watched Rhonda sweep that long silky hair over her lovely shoulder and he sighed. Oh, he wanted her desperately. He wanted to be the man in her life. He wanted to marry her and live passionately ever after.

"What does it mean to be campused?" Tony asked.

"It means not leaving the grounds at all," Rhonda said and frowned. "You have to stay in your dorm on weekends. You can go to class, to chapel, to the library, to the caf, but nowhere else. Not downtown, not to a movie, not to the cities, not anywhere."

"A whole month. Geez," Tony said.

Jon passed Rhonda the most sympathetic look he could muster, but inside he secretly rejoiced. For an entire month he wouldn't have to wonder where she was or who she was with.

Jonathan Adamson stared across the cafeteria table at Rhonda Rasmussen. She was the most gorgeous young woman he had ever seen in his entire eighteen years of life. He wanted her with the kind of passion he had only read about in pulp paperbacks. Everything in Jon's young soul said yes. Absolutely.

Just thinking about her made him twitch all over.

15

Armistice Day, November 11, 1946, was a day to celebrate. The deadliest, most expensive war of all time had come to an end at last. Weapons of unbelievable power had been used—but were now at rest. Everyone was thankful.

Although November 11 fell on a Monday, perfect for a three day holiday, St. Olaf students and faculty had a special one-hour chapel convocation but no day off. There were papers to write and books to read. The Christmas concert was less than a month away. Final exams loomed just six weeks away. Students couldn't slow down even for a national holiday as important as Armistice Day.

Jon was as busy as everyone else. He was distracted from his studies only by thoughts of Rhonda. She was stuck on campus for a month, so she wasn't hard to find—but she was seldom alone. Sometimes she ate or studied with choir members, sometimes with Holly, other times with groups of corridor mates from their dorm. Tony appeared to respect Jon's wish. He no longer ate alone with Rhonda. He only sat with her as part of a group.

Tony rarely spent time in their dorm room, so Jon began to study there most days. He often took afternoon naps too, catching up on the sleep he continued to lose because of Tony's nightmares.

Tony usually studied in the library or with other GIs, especially Flyboy. Jon tried once to join them for an English literature cram session in the Lion's Den, but so many of them smoked that afterward his eyes burned half the night.

Jon wanted desperately to spend more time with Rhonda. But because she was campused, there couldn't be any private meetings in the back booth at the bakery. And he couldn't take her anywhere in his car.

I need to get her alone somewhere, Jon thought, somewhere on campus, some intimate and private place that no one else knows about. A place where we can talk, where I can hold her in my arms.

On Friday afternoon, that second week in November, Jon slipped his flashlight in his back pocket and sauntered nonchalantly across the grass to the Finseth Bandstand. A turn-of-the-century artifact, the shell-like wooden structure, a roofed hemisphere, stood on the commons in front of Ytterboe and was seldom used.

When no one was looking, Jon ducked through the low door, snapped on his flashlight, and studied the interior. In the crawl space beneath the bandstand lay stacks of planks and risers, the bleachers that decades before had been set up in front of the band shell for summer concerts.

Cigarette butts on the dirt floor, some of them bright red with lipstick, told Jon he wasn't the only one who knew about this private place.

Jon crouched in the cramped and quiet hideaway, wondering if there, or maybe in Ytterboe attic, he and Rhonda would ever make love.

In his last year or two of high school, Jon had watched other guys in their quest for love. Downtown at Smiley's Pool Hall he'd seen guys he knew slip a quarter across the glass counter and get a three-pack of rubbers in return. Did Jon need to do that? Was he ready for that? Yikes. Would Smiley Thompson die laughing if Jonathan Adamson tried to buy rubbers?

That Friday night, Jon went home for a porkchop and gravy supper, his dad's favorite. After dinner, Jon decided he'd go to the high school football game instead of studying.

"I'll sleep here tonight," he told his mom. "Please leave the back door open for me."

Jon drove the roadster across town to Memorial Field. It was chilly now riding in the little canvas topped car.

The game was the last of the season. Northfield played Rochester. Professors' kids against Mayo Clinic doctors' kids. If she hadn't been campused, Jon might have invited Rhonda to the game. Then again, he wouldn't have wanted to risk their relationship in a high school crowd. Someone would've probably said something embarrassing or teased him for showing up with a goddess. Which she was.

Jon tried mingling with the fans in the bleachers as much as he could—without success. Being away for only a couple of months had made him an alien in his own hometown. He watched the game half-heartedly and didn't even care who won.

Jon greeted a few of the people he knew, guys he used to run around with and a couple of girls he'd dated—but they seemed so young, so small-townish—compared to Rhonda and Tony and Flyboy and Shark and Boomer and all the others. Jon was a stranger now—and he felt like one.

"How's St. Olaf?" a few of them asked.

"Great," he said, feeling like it would've been impossible to encapsulate for these young kids all that he'd seen and learned since the beginning of September. Besides, they'd never believe him.

A couple of teachers nodded and waved. Mr. Mason, his godfather and his dad's close friend, said hello. Miss Magner and Mr. Everson waved too. Jon waved back. Then he left, before the game had even ended.

Jon drove through town on his way home. He saw the kids clustered in front of Ma Gates' Cafe and Smiley's Pool Hall and they all looked so young. He stopped at the Standard station and had Lonnie put in fifty cents worth of gas.

"Big spender," Lonnie said, just as he always did.

Jon drove home. His mom and dad were out somewhere, but a plate of cookies waited for Jon on the table. He ate a few, gulped a glass of milk, and left enough of a mess so his mom would know he was home and had gone to bed.

On Saturday after supper, Jon caught up with Rhonda on her way to the library.

"How are you surviving being campused?" he asked.

"I'm bored out of my brain."

"I have a little getaway place right here on campus," he said.

"You do?"

"I'll show you."

Jon took her elbow and led her across the grass to the back of the bandstand. He stood in the doorway, lit a match, and led her inside.

"Watch your head," he warned.

Rhonda looked around at the cramped space, the open studs on the wall, the joists and bandstand floorboards overhead.

"It's not the Ritz-Palladium," she said, "but like you say, it's private. It certainly is that."

"How about meeting me here tonight?" Jon suggested. "We can talk."

"I have to cram at the library until it closes. I could meet you here at ten, but only for a little while. I have to be in by 10:30. That's curfew when you're campused, even on a weekend night."

"I'll be here," Jon said. He squeezed her hand quickly and they slipped out.

Back in his room, Jon had an impossible time studying. He paced dozens of laps across the length of the room, his research manual in hand. He had to footnote several unpublished letters in his English term paper and couldn't find the proper form. Worst of all, he couldn't concentrate. Not when he was going to meet Rhonda at the band shell in less than two hours.

Suddenly Jon had to go to the bathroom. He laid his grammar book face down on his desk top, but the binding was so new the book wouldn't stay open. Not wanting to lose his page, he glanced around for a bookmark.

Holding his grammar book in one hand, he leaned over and checked Tony's wastebasket for a scrap of paper.

On top of the heap of trash was a folded envelope. Just right for a bookmark, Jon thought. He picked it up and was about to slide it into the book when he realized it wasn't empty. He clamped the open book between his knees and used both hands to inspect the envelope's contents.

Inside was a slithery rubber. Used.

Jon stared at the condom. When had Tony used that? he wondered. And on whom? And where? Here? Geez.

Jon folded the envelope, concealing the gooey thing once again, and laid it back in the wastebasket.

He walked back to his desk slowly and sat down hard. He stared at the page of punctuation rules in his grammar book but his eyes were drawn back, again and again, to the wastebasket.

He walked to the window and saw a few wisps of snow fall from the sky. The first of the season. Jon checked his watch again, then remembered suddenly his forgotten trip to the bathroom. He set his Land-O-Lakes crock on top of his grammar book to hold it open and went down the hall.

At five minutes to ten, Jon slipped on his coat and put a candle and a book of matches in his pocket. He ran across the grass, snowflakes stinging his cheeks, and ducked inside the band shell. He lit a candle and secured it with melted wax to a crossbrace on the wall.

He sat on a pile of planks and waited.

He sat and waited some more.

Jon checked his watch every thirty seconds and chewed on the corner of the matchbook in-between.

At 10:20 he sighed. Devastated, he jammed the soggy matchbook into his pocket and stood up.

He puckered his lips to blow out the candle when suddenly Rhonda ducked in the low door.

Jon dropped back onto his makeshift plank bench.

"I'm sorry," she said. "I ran into my music theory teacher's assistant. I asked him so many questions that we were the last ones out of the library." She looked around. "Candlelight," she murmured and smiled. "Isn't this romantic."

Rhonda sat down beside Jon on the planks and gazed at him. He smiled, trying hard to hide his tremendous relief.

They sat in silence for several minutes.

Suddenly Jon couldn't stand it any longer. He wrapped his arms around her, pulled her toward him, and kissed her. She melted into him, kissing him deeply in return.

"That was nice," she said, pulling away from him.

She took his left hand in hers. He hoped fleetingly that she was drawing his hand over to lay on her breast. Instead, she turned his wrist toward the burning candle.

"Oh, boy," she said, staring at his watch for a second. "When you're campused you don't dare be even one second late." She leaned over and kissed him quickly on the lips, then ducked out the door.

Jon blew out the candle and shook the hot wax off the top, grinning so broadly his face ached.

He floated back to room 223, Ytterboe Hall. Tony stood in the hallway pulling their door shut as Jon appeared.

"I'm heading downtown," Tony said. "Hey, there was a phone call for you. Your grandma died. Brinkley? Is that the name?"

"Brindley. Grandma Brindley," Jon said, tears brimming up against his will and filling his eyes.

"I'm sorry," Tony said. "Anything I can do?"

"No," Jon said. "No, thanks."

Although Grandma Brindley had ancestors on the Mayflower and had been a lifelong Anglican, the family decided to have the funeral at the Adamsons' church in Northfield, St. John's Lutheran.

After the service, Jon saw Tony moving toward him across the narthex. Jon had told Tony about the funeral but he never expected him to appear. He was even wearing a tie.

"It was really nice of you to come," Jon said, sincerely touched by the gesture.

"No sweat," Tony said and shrugged.

"There's my sister, Trudy. I'd like you to meet her."

"Sure," Tony said.

Jon called Trudy over and she offered her hand, shaking Tony's firmly. She'd learned to shake hands from their father. No dead fish, he always said.

"So you're Tony," Trudy said. "Jon told me you made the St. Olaf Choir. Congratulations."

"Thanks. You sang in the choir too, I hear."

"Yes. All four years. Now I'm studying in New York. Dr. Christiansen has recommended me for Robert Shaw's Collegiate Chorale."

"Terrific. And your solo today was great. Sorry about your grandma," Tony added.

"She was a real sweetheart," Trudy said. "She liked Jon best, though," she added, nudging Jon teasingly. "Are you coming downstairs for coffee?" she asked Tony.

"I told Flyboy I'd meet him at the front door."

"Flyboy?" Trudy asked.

"A classmate," Tony explained. "He's picking me up here. We're going to the cities for the afternoon."

"Come on downstairs, Tony," Jon said. "Flyboy will find you there."

Downstairs, Tony stood in line and expressed sympathy to Jon's parents. Then he filled a plate with Ladies' Aid funeral food and joined Jon and Trudy at a table.

"I hear you and Jon had quite a Halloween," Trudy said to Tony, smiling.

"That's right," Tony replied, inhaling a whole ham salad tea sandwich in one swallow.

"You have to take better care of my little brother," Trudy said, patting Jon's cheek. "He's pretty innocent."

He swatted her hand away, wanting desperately to change the subject.

Just then, rotund Uncle Lars squeezed into the chair across from Tony.

"Who the hell is *this*," Lars bellowed, nodding at Tony. "He's not Norwegian."

"This is my roommate, Tony Tarpezi," Jon said. Tony stood up and shook Lars's hand. "This is my uncle, Lars Gustavson. He works for 3M."

"Tony, good to meetcha," Uncle Lars boomed, banging his empty coffee cup on the table. "Italian, right?" Lars asked. Tony nodded. "I knew you weren't Norwegian."

Jon watched Uncle Lars slip a silver flask out of his inside pocket and pour a generous dose into his cup.

"Tony was in Italy at the tail end of the war," Jon said to Uncle Lars. "He's a vet."

"No kidding," Lars boomed.

"Yeah," Tony said, nodding. "My outfit went through there."

"You have any relatives still living in Italy?" Lars asked.

"Not that I know of."

"Well, listen to this. Minnesota M & M is going to set up plants in Italy within the next few years. My division. Abrasives. If you had relatives over there, we could give you a job."

"I graduate in four years. I'll look you up the day after commencement," Tony said. "By then I'll have cooked up all the relatives you need."

"Oh, I like that," Lars said, elbowing Jon. "He's good." He took a long drink from his cup, then said to Tony, "Be sure to take business administration courses."

"I plan on it," Tony replied.

"Keep in touch, Tony, will you?" Uncle Lars said and stood up. He boomed a goodbye, then moved to the next table. Wherever Uncle Lars traveled, the sound level and laughter escalated.

Just then, Jon spotted Flyboy. He was peering into the room, cautiously, from the front stairwell. He appeared to be scouring the crowd for some sign of Tony.

Jon caught Flyboy's eye and waved him over, beckoning him to join them.

Flyboy shook his head. Tony jumped up, said goodbye to Trudy, slugged Jon on the shoulder, and trotted off to the door. He waved at Uncle Lars on the way out.

Jon noticed Trudy gawking.

"Interesting, isn't he?"

"Is he ever—and such chiseled features too."

"Tony?"

"No, the one in the flight jacket."

"That's Flyboy."

"He's dreamy. What's his real name?"

"His last name is Paulsrud," Jon replied. He had to think about the first name. It wasn't Scandinavian like Paulsrud. It wasn't Nordic at all, as Jon remembered. More Irish, he recalled.

Kelly. That was it.

"Paulsrud," Jon said. "Kelly Paulsrud."

"What a beautiful name. He looks like a Norse god," Trudy said and sighed.

Jon shook his head and thought, *What next.*

16

"Thanks again for coming to the funeral yesterday," Jon said.

"I can't say it was my pleasure," Tony grumbled, "except for your sister's solo."

Jon sighed. He'd seen a gracious side in Tony at the funeral, but the grey November day had him back in his standard grumpy form.

"Do you know who Trudy thought was dreamy looking—and from fifty paces?"

"Me?"

"No. Flyboy."

"You're kidding. Holy shit." His mood had suddenly changed again, and a hint of excitement flavored his voice. "Well, someone like Trudy is just what Flyboy needs. He's like you, Flyboy is. Underneath he's an exact replica of you. Innocent as hell."

"What was he doing with Gloria Tanager, then?"

"That was the fighter pilot in him. Even *I* can't imagine what that was like. Flying was triple-shit worse than the tank corps, especially for fighter pilots. If it wasn't the enemy, it was the damn airplanes. Flyboy said a third of the casualties in his unit were because of plane failure. Early in the war they were patching planes together with chewing gum." He paused and pulled an ear lobe. "So Trudy really likes Flyboy?"

"She likes the way he looks, that's all she said."

"He'd like the way *she* looks. Your sister's a fox. I think they should meet, I really do. It's time for Flyboy to quit being a fucked-up fighter pilot and go back to being an Iowa farm kid."

"Where is he from in Iowa?"

"I can't remember. Some border town."

Tony looked at his watch. He wound it a few turns, then said, "I have to go. Rehearsal."

"Say hi to Rhonda for me, okay?"

"Sure," Tony agreed. He walked out the door then turned back and said, "*She* should give up being a fighter pilot, too."

"What does that mean?"

"Nothing. See you later," he said and clicked the door shut.

The three weeks between Grandma Brindley's funeral and the Christmas concert flew by. Jon studied day and night. Tony practiced almost constantly with the choir.

Rhonda, too, was beyond busy. Again and again, Jon tried to find a time to be alone with her, to eat together, to slip below the band shell together, to do *anything* together. But the most they could manage in those three weeks were a few meals in groups and a few hurried walks across campus between classes.

On Monday of Christmas festival week, the tension permeated the whole campus. Having gone to the St. Olaf Christmas concert every December since he was a small boy, Jon knew the annual ritual like he knew the alphabet. The Christmas concert weekend was always the same. St. Olaf College put on her native costume and invited thousands of people to come and savor the old-country ways. The cafeteria served a lavish Scandinavian smorgasbord—lutefisk and lefse, Swedish meatballs, herring, rommegrot, rice pudding, and Norwegian Christmas cookies, such as fattigman and sandbakkels. Waitresses in Scandinavian costume—red dresses, poofy white blouses, and black vests—served oceans of coffee.

The concert itself was always beautiful and moving. Every year it ended with F. Melius Christiansen's *Beautiful Savior*. Old graduates who were back, especially choir alumni, always cried at that point. After the concert, especially on Sunday night, senior singers hugged each other and also cried, knowing it was their last concert ever.

Being a townie, the dean's kid, and the younger brother of a choir member, Jon knew plenty about this yearly ritual. He also knew that sneaking in to the strictly closed Thursday night dress rehearsal was taboo—therefore, a risk.

After supper Thursday night, Jon meandered across campus to the gymnasium. When no one was looking, he darted through the lobby and up a flight of stairs to the second level wrestling room. He tiptoed through the dark, deserted room and through the door to the running track. He crept along the cork track and sat down in the shadows under the bleachers.

His eyes quickly adjusted to the dim light and he fixed them on one focal point: Rhonda. She looked so lovely, so angelic across the darkened gymnasium. She sang the manger story and looked like a reincarnation of the Virgin Mary. Then the next moment Jon saw a different Rhonda, her lips hard against his, her tan breasts on display through her open robe. Wow.

Jon stared solely at Rhonda for more than a half hour. He finally managed to pull his eyes away and glance at the other choir and orchestra members. All of the singers looked saintly singing those Christmas anthems, Jon realized. Even Tony. Give Gloria Tanager a resonant alto voice and she'd be in too, Jon supposed. And voluptuously available to entertain the troops on choir tour.

Whatever chemistry made this musical magic happen, Jon thought, it worked superbly. The Christmas concert was the highlight of the whole year on Manitou Heights.

After the rehearsal, singers from all of the choirs mingled in the lobby. Jon stole back downstairs and searched for Rhonda in the crowd. He wanted to share this special time with her, to walk her home too, and maybe duck into their band shell getaway together.

He finally spotted her down the hall. She leaned against a wall and was engaged in an animated conversation with one of the senior soloists, her sparkling eyes locked to his. They stood so close that the hems of their purple robes were intertwined.

Jon stared in jealous confusion.

Suddenly Tony, still in his purple robe, appeared beside Jon. "Give her up, kid," he whispered in Jon's ear. "She'd never be anything but pain."

"Shut up," Jon growled. He ran out into the cold night.

On Friday morning, Rhonda called to Jon outside the library. "Hi, Jon," she said breezily. "Didn't I see you after dress rehearsal last night?"

Jon nodded. "I watched the whole rehearsal," he said, silently ordering his voice to be steady. "And I watched you afterward with Halvor Follensby."

"Doesn't he have the most beautiful voice?"

"So what color are his eyes?"

"Come on, Jon. We were just talking."

Jon stared at her and sighed. Her extraordinary beauty overwhelmed him.

She smiled then, so warmly, so sweetly. Jon felt his bitterness wane, then wash thoroughly away.

"So when are you planning to see the concert?" she asked.

"I have tickets for Sunday."

"Why don't you take Holly? She just told me she's having some trouble with her family. She really needs to get out."

"I'd rather take you."

"You want to stand up there beside me on the risers?" she said, laughing, "and pretend you're singing?" Rhonda ran off for class then, leaving Jon feeling confused again and longing desperately for her.

At supper that evening, Jon asked Holly to the Sunday concert. He figured he'd earn points with Rhonda if he did.

"Thanks," Holly said with a sad look in her eye. "My parents won't be coming this year."

Jon asked why but she wouldn't say. She changed the subject to the weather and finals, and the conversation remained focused on snowflakes and study strategies until the end of the meal.

Jon waited for Holly just inside Agnes Mellby's main door on Sunday evening. When she appeared he could see she'd been crying. Her eyes were red.

"What's wrong, Holly?" he asked.

"Nothing."

"It's *not* nothing," Jon insisted. "What's wrong? Come on, tell me. Should we go into the lounge?"

"Can we just leave?"

Jon helped her put on her coat and pushed open Mellby Hall's medieval oak front door. The minute they were out in the cold air, Holly started to cry again. The moon reflecting off the snow made the tears glisten on her cheeks.

Jon stopped, put his hands on her shoulders, and turned her toward him. "Tell me," he insisted.

"I just had another phone call from home," she said and wiped her nose in a tissue. "It's a family thing. There's nothing you can do."

"How do we know that unless you tell me?"

"Listen," Holly stopped suddenly and said, "do you mind going alone? I won't be good company."

"We don't have to go at all," Jon said firmly. "*I* don't have to go." Is this me saying this? he thought. He quickly weighed the loss of not watching Rhonda sing in a real performance—and the last performance of the season at that—against the gain of doing as Rhonda suggested, to be of some help and comfort to Holly.

"That's not fair," Holly said. "You shouldn't have to miss the concert."

"I saw the whole dress rehearsal," he argued. "Besides, I've seen it lots of times."

"Tony and Rhonda are in it. You need to go. Go without me, okay? Please."

Holly started crying harder, tore away from Jon's grip, and ran back toward the dorm. Jon practically tackled her to get her to stop.

"Let's just walk—or better yet, let's go to my house," he said. "We can talk there."

"I don't want to see your parents. I don't want to see anybody."

"There's no one home. My parents are in Minneapolis overnight, cleaning out my grandma's house and packing up all her things."

Something Jon said made Holly start to cry again.

Jon put his arm around her as they walked. "All right, what is it?" he asked.

"We're packing too. My dad lost his job. We have to move before Christmas."

"Where? Move where?"

"I don't know where. But worse than that, I have to drop out of college."

"How does a pastor lose his job, for pete's sake?"

"It's a long story."

"When we get to my house, I want you to tell me everything."

They walked the rest of the way down St. Olaf Avenue and over to Second Street in silence. Jon stepped inside his parents' garage, patted his car twice on the fender, and pulled a house key out of a flower pot. Jon suddenly remembered his father's words spoken just a day earlier and with a smile: "No wild parties while we're gone. Keep your nose clean."

Jon had agreed, also with a smile.

They both knew he wouldn't take advantage of their absence. But Jon was sure his parents wouldn't mind if he had Holly in. His mom especially would think it was the right thing to do for Holly when she was so miserable.

Jon unlocked the back door and led Holly into the kitchen. He turned the light on over the kitchen sink, then walked into the living room and turned up the thermostat. He heard the furnace kick in. With only the one light on, the kitchen felt cozy and comforting.

Jon helped Holly out of her coat and offered her a chair at the kitchen table. She shivered.

"Would you like something warm to drink?" he asked. "Tea? Coffee? Or maybe you'd rather have a Coke."

"How about something strong," Holly said. "Something like that sloe gin we had at the bakery."

"Really? I can look, I guess."

Jon opened the cupboard under the sink. His parents seldom drank anything, but every Christmas his father got a fancy looking bottle of liquor from Sid Freeman. Jon's dad bowled on a team sponsored by Sid's clothing store. Years' worth of bottles had collected under the sink, most of them unopened.

"What would you like?" Jon asked, dropping to his knees and reading the labels. "Brandy? Whiskey?"

"What do I know?" Holly said with a sniff. "You choose."

Jon pulled out a bottle of brandy that had already been opened, stood up, and set it on the counter. "I'd better mix it with Coke or something," he said.

He popped the cap off a cold bottle of Coke. He'd never mixed a drink before. How much brandy should he add? He poured in about the same amount Tony had used at the bakery.

Jon handed her the drink and watched it disappear in less than a minute.

"Can you make me another?" Holly asked.

"I guess so. But I really don't think you should have any more."

"Well, I do," she said, jumping up and mixing her second one even stronger. She took a gulp and mumbled, "I can't believe they'd do that to my dad."

She dropped back into her chair and quickly gulped the rest of her second drink. Jon studied her pretty face and blond hair, realizing suddenly how little he'd seen of her since Halloween.

"Tell me about your dad's job."

"He's been there more than twelve years. I started school in Forest Mills. We've lived there since I was six. It's my hometown. Most of my friends belong to that church. They threw him out." She spoke more and more slowly, her eyes beginning to look glazed.

"What did he do?"

"Told the truth, that's all."

"About what?"

"About everything—but mostly about Hiroshima and Nagasaki."

"You mean he preached against the atomic bomb?"

"He started a series of sermons last August, on the first anniversary of Hiroshima. He said it was wrong. He said that our children and grandchildren would blame us for that decision. He mentioned it in almost every sermon this fall. He knew it would bother some people, especially some of the veterans, but he thought they would at least respect his opinion. Last week the church council met secretly and voted him out. They asked him to resign." Holly spat her words angrily throughout her soliloquy and began to appear unsteady on her chair.

"Will he do it? Will he leave without a fight?"

"He resigned instantly. My dad wouldn't stay where he's not wanted."

"Boy," Jon said, shaking his head.

"The council is only eight men. What makes me really furious is the rest of the church. He served all those people for twelve years and really cared for them and now they turn on him like a pack of jackals. They pulled him down just like animals would," she blurted and tried to snap her fingers but her coordination was gone. The completely put together Holly Hanson was coming apart, unstrung by brandy Cokes.

It suddenly occurred to Jon what Tony would say, that all this was happening in the DEAN's kitchen. He was getting an under-age St. Olaf student drunk on the DEAN's liquor, in the DEAN's house. He could just hear Tony saying it. Jon was breaking school rules, the state law, and his promise to his father.

Not only that, but he and Holly were alone in the house. That wouldn't look good if anyone found out.

"I have to take you back to campus, Holly," Jon said. "Right now. Or we could get in big trouble."

"I don't mind getting in trouble, especially if I'm with you. What I don't want to do is go back to that damn *Lutheran* school."

Holly slurred "Lutheran" so violently that the big OOOO at the beginning sounded just like Tony's frequent sarcastic pronunciation of the word.

"Another brandy and Coke, please, handsome waiter, and no ice," she added in a thick slur.

"No more," Jon said. "You've had enough."

"Well. . .then. . .I'll mix it myself." Holly staggered to a standing position and made her way haltingly over to the counter to mix another drink.

Jon jumped up and grabbed the bottle out of her hand. He pulled Holly down into her chair, then put the bottle back under the sink and shut the cupboard door firmly.

"Wait right there, *please*," he said, his hands held high and his palms opened wide in a calm down gesture. "I have to make a phone call."

Jon had to find someone who could meet them on campus and help Holly back into her dorm, a female student who could sneak Holly in and put her to bed. But who? Everyone Jon knew was either singing in the concert or attending it.

Jon tried calling Sarah, Trudy's friend. She was a senior and would know what to do. Someone answered on her floor and said Sarah was at the Christmas concert.

Though he knew her only from the Halloween party, Jon tried Joyce Kensington, the navy pilot. She was out of town.

I'll have to sneak Holly back in myself, Jon thought. But he had no idea how he'd accomplish that. If he was caught in the girls' dorm with an inebriated girl, he could kiss his college diploma goodbye.

Jon turned back to the kitchen and blinked in surprise. The brandy bottle was back on the counter, the lid off. The cupboard door stood open.

Then Jon saw Holly. She stood beside her chair, rocking slowly and threatening to topple over. Her blouse was on the floor. The top half of her slip hung down around her hips. She was sliding a bra strap down over her shoulder. Jon was shocked motionless. He wanted to stop her but he couldn't move.

"I know I can't be Rhonda," she managed to say in her slurred voice, "but I could be like Gloria Tanager. Tonight I want to break all the rules."

Jon just stood there and stared.

"What good is that goddam church and all its rules? Hypocripps. . .hypocricks. . .hickopricks. . ." Her numb tongue made the pronunciation of hypocrites impossible.

"Holly," Jon said and shook his head. "Sweet, pretty Holly. You don't want to be doing this."

"Yes, I do. I don't want to be a good, little virgin anymore—and you're the only one I can trust." Virgin had so many syllables and glottal stops the way she pronounced the word, that it sounded like Japanese.

Jon didn't have to argue with her any more. Suddenly she sank in a heap onto the linoleum. She was out cold.

Jon didn't know what to do. Would she be okay? He'd heard of people dying from alcohol poisoning. Two of his friends had polished off about the same amount of liquor on a camping trip and had survived, but Holly was a girl—and half their size and weight.

He decided to put her to bed and watch her carefully for awhile. He figured he could call an ambulance if he had to. He thought about how *that* would look—flashing lights, a half-naked female student being carried out of the dean's house. But Jon knew he didn't have a choice.

He threw her blouse over his shoulder and knelt down to pick her up. She looked astonishingly beautiful lying there on her back, her knees leaning over to one side. He noticed the horizontal sun-tan line of her summer swim suit across the top half of her white breasts, a line, he thought, as inviolable as an international border.

Jon was certain he was the very first male—other than Holly's family doctor—who'd ever seen her with her shirt off.

He sighed, rolled her into his arms, and staggered a little as he stood up. He carried her into Trudy's bedroom, careful of Holly's head in the doorway. He laid her on the bed, took off her shoes, and began to rub her small feet briskly, for what reason he wasn't exactly sure—maybe to keep her blood flowing.

He covered her with a blanket, then pulled up a chair along-side the bed.

He studied her face. She looked so relaxed, so soft. He won-dered if she might get sick. If she did, he'd have to wash the sheets, the blankets, the carpet—everything very carefully so his parents wouldn't find out.

Jon leaned over Trudy's desk and grabbed her wastebasket. Holly could be sick in that if she had to.

He watched over Holly until long past midnight. She didn't get sick. She slept soundly, although breathing so deeply and slowly at times, that Jon felt afraid and often found himself hold-ing his own breath waiting for *her* to exhale. When he bent down to check her, she smelled volatile.

It was now the middle of the night and Jon knew her body was still kicking off the poison. Vile stuff.

Jon spent the rest of the night curled up in Trudy's desk chair. He napped fitfully, only in snatches. He awoke at seven o'clock in the morning with a painfully stiff neck. Oh, boy.

Holly awakened minutes later. Her hands moved under the blanket and she discovered that her blouse was gone. She looked at Jon angrily.

"What did we do?" she demanded.

"Nothing."

"Are you sure?"

"I wouldn't forget something like that."

"What did I say?"

"Plenty. How do you feel?"

"My head really hurts," she said with a scowl, rubbing her temples.

"I'll get you some aspirin and water, then I'll make coffee. When is your first class?"

"At eight-fifty. I have to go."

"I do, too. You need to get back to your dorm right away. I think we should both pray that the housemother didn't do a bed check last night. Look in Trudy's closet, why don't you," Jon said, pointing. "You can't go to class in that wrinkled outfit."

Holly's hands moved over her bare skin again. She managed a feeble half smile and whispered, "Thanks, Jon."

Jon smiled back, turned away, and dragged himself to the kitchen, feeling very sore and confused.

He measured spoons of coffee grounds into the pot and thought to himself, Once upon a time I believed what I'd learn in college would come from books and lectures.

17

With the Christmas concert over, Jon hoped Rhonda would have more time for him. He caught up with her after chapel on Tuesday.

"Are things quieting down now that the concert's over?" Jon asked her.

"Don't I wish. Exams are coming up and I have to work the Christmas rush at the bakery."

"They're not open nights, though," Jon said. "I hoped we could do something together Friday or Saturday, just the two of us."

"Oh, Jon, you know I'd love to," she said and rubbed Jon's cheek gently with the back of her soft hand, giving Jon tingles. "Trouble is, I'm auditioning for a part in a summer play at the Old Log Theater on Friday, so I'm spending the night at my grandmother's in Edina. It's my first free weekend since I was campused."

"I could meet you there," Jon said. "I know where it is."

"We'd better not. I don't know how involved I'll get with the audition."

"Saturday, then?" Jon asked.

"Saturday's reading day," Rhonda said. "With the concert and all, I'm just so far behind. I really have to study."

Jon's disappointed look must have been obvious.

"We can try to do something next week," she added, then ran off to class.

On the Friday after the Christmas concert's grand finale, students found themselves already thinking about spring, in spite of the snow, wool coats, and subzero temperatures. Friday, December 13, 1946, was registration day for spring term classes.

That morning Tony woke Jon early.

"This is it," he said. "Get up, Jon. Time to go to the gym."

"I don't register until ten-thirty," Jon said and yawned widely.

"That's the whole idea," Tony said. "We get in early."

"Meaning?" Jon asked.

"You'll find out. Just get on your jeans and a shirt, then put these coveralls over top. Come on," Tony said, handing Jon a pair of army surplus coveralls.

Jon slipped into the coveralls, thinking of the hours he and his father had spent shopping for tools in military surplus stores. These shops had popped up everywhere in 1946, selling leftover wartime equipment and clothing—knives, machetes, olive drab fatigues, tents, jungle hammocks, camp stoves, boots, skis, snowshoes, tools, K-rations. Entrepreneurs bought tons of leftover army and navy supplies for next to nothing in truckload lots, marked them up two thousand per cent, and sold them in surplus stores.

"What if it doesn't work?" Jon asked, buttoning his coveralls.

"It'll work. Just roll up your pants, for God's sake," Tony said, pointing at the cuffs of Jon's coveralls. "You look like Charlie Chaplin."

Jon could see his questions were irritating Tony. He decided just to listen and do what he was told. There were a couple of popular classes he really wanted, so Jon hoped Tony's plan would work. He quickly bent down and rolled up his cuffs.

"We can wear hats and gloves but not coats. I want to have the full visual effect of these coveralls. Can you survive the deep freeze out there for a few hundred yards without a coat?"

"Sure," Jon said, tugging on his navy skullcap.

"Good. Let's go, then," Tony said, checking his watch for the tenth time. "Do you have all your registration forms?"

Jon nodded.

"This is our chance to get even with the system," Tony said, "not to mention that frickin' gestapo bunch in the registrar's office."

They picked up the toilet and carried it between them. Tony used only his right hand. "No need for a two-by-four this short distance," he said. "The gym doors open at eight o'clock," he added as they walked out Ytterboe's front door. "We need to get there by 8:04, right after everyone else goes in. I have this deal timed to the split second. You know, like a counterattack. Then voilá, we get to register with the first group."

"Even though we're supposed to register at ten-thirty?"

"Yup."

"Gotcha."

They carried the toilet five hundred yards to the door of the gym, in fifteen degrees below zero winds. It was a December morning just as unseasonably cold as the stretch in September had been unseasonably hot.

At exactly 8:04 by Jon's watch, he and Tony moved into the lobby of the gym with the toilet between them. They quickly crossed the lobby and moved boldly through the doors and into the gym.

"The plumbing shop asked us to carry this toilet to the rest room," Tony lied to Professor Huggenvik who stood guard at the open double doors.

"Glad to see you doing something useful, Adamson," Huggenvik said as Tony and Jon walked by.

Jon smiled, swallowing his guilt for taking part in a lie. He marched along behind Tony, the toilet between them, preparing to accept as gracefully as possible another probation sentence if they got caught.

"That was a lead-pipe cinch," Tony whispered as they turned and headed briskly toward the rest rooms. The women's room was twenty feet nearer than the men's. Tony stopped abruptly, knocked twice on the women's room door, pushed it open, and shouted, "Plumbers!"

Then he walked in.

"Are you *crazy?*" Jon hissed. They set the toilet in the middle of the white tiled floor.

"I figure it would be more fun to make our clothes-switch in the chicks' john."

"Fun?" Jon said, anxiously scanning the room for any sign of a female.

It appeared to be empty.

"Why would anyone come in here," Tony said, "when she could be out there getting her pick of the best courses?"

"I don't know," Jon whispered, "but I hear her coming."

"Quick. In here." Tony pulled Jon into the nearest stall and snapped the lock shut.

Without making a sound, Jon quickly lowered the toilet lid and jumped onto it. He shuffled back, making room for Tony, who jumped up just as quickly. They crouched down and Jon nearly gasped as Tony's weight squished him against the wall.

They huddled there like trapped rats, listening and waiting noiselessly.

"What's this?" a female voice asked and giggled. "Look. A toilet in the middle of the floor."

"Strange," said another voice. Jon recognized Holly's voice instantly. He hadn't talked to her since their Sunday night brandy Coke fiasco. He'd seen her in the caf and in the library, but she seemed to be purposely avoiding eye contact with him. Jon figured she was embarrassed.

"I can't believe I have to waste time in the bathroom," said the other girl. "I luck out and get first group registration and then catch a dose of TB."

"TB?" Holly asked, sounding puzzled.

"Tiny bladder. I've *really* got to *go.*"

The girl fiddled with the locked door just inches from Tony's nose. Jon's heart almost stopped. Without questioning, the girl scurried on to the next stall.

"Of all the dumb times," Holly said. "My stupid bra strap broke when I took my coat off in the lobby. Too much of a hurry, I guess."

Jon felt his face grow warm with embarrassment, hearing the other girl go to the bathroom.

"Do you need any help with your bra?" she asked as she flushed the toilet.

"No, thanks," Holly said.

"I hope no one else comes in while you're standing there with your shirt off," the other girl said and laughed. "Bye!" She left the rest room and the door banged shut behind her.

Tony twisted his neck around and looked at Jon. He raised his eyebrows several times, Groucho style. Then he faced forward again and started to crane his neck upward to peer over the stall door.

Jon grabbed the neck of Tony's coveralls and firmly held him down.

Tony shrugged him off, but he stayed put.

Holly finally left and they stepped off the stool.

"We missed the chance of a lifetime," Tony said and smirked, nudging Jon with his elbow. "You know who that was, don't you?"

"Yes. Holly."

"I'll bet she looks great with her shirt off," Tony said with a grin and a quick dance of his eyebrows.

Jon nodded—more knowingly than Tony could ever have guessed.

"She would've died if she'd seen us," Jon said. "And it would've been the end of your grand plan if we'd been caught in here."

"I guess you're right," Tony agreed. "Well, time to strip for action."

They scrambled out of their coveralls, rolled them into balls and shoved them under handfuls of paper towel in the waste can.

Tony peeked out the door, then whispered, "Come on. Fast."

He darted out of the women's rest room and stopped at an empty table ten feet away. Jon followed. They stood there, pretending to study a stack of registration forms, then Tony strolled off nonchalantly toward the registration tables. Jon waited another minute, then stepped out and joined the crowd.

He tried his best to appear invisible. It wasn't so easy since most of the faculty had known him since he was a toddler.

Jon moved from table to table, getting his registration card stamped. Tony was right. It was a cinch. Jon was snagging every class and every prof he'd hoped for.

Whenever Jon saw Miss Thorsgaard coming his way, he buried his head in his catalog or bent over his registration form and pretended to be writing. He knew it would be all over if she spotted him there that early.

She saw Tony, though. Jon listened in.

"Well," she said to Tony, "did you get into a biology class this time, Mr. . . Mr. . ."

She's forgotten his name, Jon thought. That's sheer luck. Jon's dad once told Jon that Miss Thorsgaard's memory was keener than a reference librarian's.

"Mr. Garpezi," Tony replied, hitting the G hard. "Getting to register first this semester," he added, "suits me to a T."

Jon quickly covered his mouth with his catalog to smother a laugh.

Tony and Jon left the gym separately and met at their room five minutes later.

"Brilliant," Jon said to his grinning roommate.

"Thank you very much," Tony said, taking a deep bow. "Now all we have to do is wander back to the gym at our scheduled time and get our courses logged in."

"Let's go have an Ole roll to celebrate," Jon suggested.

"Great idea."

They headed down the snow-covered hill to the Ole Store Cafe on St. Olaf Avenue.

Tony wolfed down his second caramel pecan roll, then stared at his registration card as he slurped his coffee.

"So what are you taking?" he asked.

"Religion," Jon said, "another history course, economics, music appreciation, and German."

"German? I thought you were Norwegian."

"I'm majoring in history, and I think I'll probably want to specialize in this century. That means I should learn German or Russian or Japanese. And they only teach German here."

"You have your life so damn figured out. I suppose you know who you'll marry, how many kids you'll have, what university you'll teach at, and how long you'll live."

"Rhonda, four, and Harvard," Jon said, "and. . .eighty-seven years, four months, and eight days—and I'm going to die water-skiing."

Tony laughed and took another slurp of coffee.

"Do you really have your life all planned out?" he asked.

"I wish I did."

"I think life needs surprises."

"Like dragging me into the girls' bathroom," Jon said with a phony scowl.

"If you hadn't been such a little chicken shit, we could have feasted our eyes on Holly Hanson's headlights."

Jon didn't respond. Tony would never guess that Jon had already come very close to experiencing that.

"I think you like Holly more than you know," Tony said.

"Sure I like her. And respect her, too. She's going through a lot right now. Her dad's changing jobs."

"You were right about us not looking, now that I think about it," Tony said. "Holly isn't the type to parade around with her nips flapping in the wind. Now if that had been Rhonda. . ."

What does he know about Rhonda? Jon thought angrily. Why does he always have to bring her into it?

"Don't get so rabid, kid," Tony said. "I wish you'd listen to me. Rhonda's no good for you."

Jon jumped up. He tossed some coins on the booth top and stormed out of the cafe.

He ran all the way back to the gym and was first in line to register with his pre-scheduled group. He hoped he wouldn't run into Tony. He needed time to cool off first.

Jon went straight to the registrar's table to have his courses logged in. He held his breath as the assistant read his registration card.

"Three of these courses have been closed since early this morning," she muttered. She looked at the blackboard to double check, then turned back to Jon and winked. "Used a little pull, did you, Jon?" she said, stamping his finished card firmly and sending him along to the treasurer's table.

Jon went to lunch feeling like he'd won the Irish Sweepstakes.

Jon walked into the cafeteria and filled his tray. Flyboy waved, beckoning Jon to join him at his table. Sitting with Flyboy carried the risk of Tony's joining them as well and he was the last person Jon wanted to see after what he'd said about Rhonda. But Flyboy was insistent.

"How did you two get in early anyway?" Flyboy asked, nodding in the direction of the gymnasium. "Tony was supposed to register with my group."

"We pretended to be plumbers. We put on army surplus coveralls and carried in that old toilet we had in our room."

He began to laugh. "You got all the good courses then."

"Sure did," Jon said. "How about you?"

"Yeah. Most of what I wanted. Flight school took care of a lot of my graduation requirements," he replied, "so I'm already working on my major. Art courses mostly—drawing, sculpture, and art history."

"You want to be an artist?"

"Art teacher, I think."

"That doesn't fit your image, somehow," Jon said. "I thought you'd want to be a test pilot, or fly a commercial plane."

"I'd buzz church steeples and fly under bridges. It'd make the passengers nervous."

"So you're from Iowa," Jon said. "Does your family farm or what?"

"Dairy. What else?"

"But you want to be an art teacher."

"My brothers will take over the farm."

They ate quietly for awhile, then Jon asked, "Do your brothers have Irish first names, too?"

"No. They're dripping in lutefisk juice, all of them. My older brothers are named Ole and Peder, can you believe it? Peder's even spelled with a 'd'. My sister's named Gudrun and she married a guy named Sigurd, if you can believe that. Sigurd and Gudrun. Sounds like a Grieg opera. We're Norwegian Iowa farmers to the very marrow of our bones."

Jon stole a glance at Kelly Paulsrud. He was undeniably handsome. Jon knew that Trudy had seen that right away.

"You older guys on campus are all kind of, well," Jon thought for a second, then admitted, "just a little intimidating."

"We're not really that much older—we just aged faster. We've been through a lot."

"Were you ever shot down—or shot up?" Jon asked and laughed at his own pun. So did Flyboy.

"Both," he said, chuckling.

"Do you ever talk about it?" Jon asked, picking at the corned beef hash on his plate.

"Sometimes. After about my fifth or sixth beer."

"It must be hard to come back from war to a place as tame as St. Olaf."

"I like St. Olaf," Flyboy said, "and I don't mind the place being so bland. Good spot to unload our springs, to unwind."

"Some people don't need a war to get wound up," Jon said.

"Like Gloria Tanager," Flyboy said with a smirk.

"Yeah. Like her. Did she go home or what?"

"She should have. She's still in Northfield, living in an apartment."

"By herself?"

"During the day," he replied, arching his eyebrows.

"I thought she was your girl," Jon said.

"I could never take a girl like that home to Iowa."

"She's not your typical dairy farm type," Jon said, emphasizing the point by clinking his glass of milk with his fingernail.

"Somebody like Holly Hanson," Flyboy said, "that would be different. My mom would eat her up."

"My mom probably would too. I guess moms are all alike."

"Yeah. Someone like Holly would weave right into the fabric of our family," Flyboy said. "And according to Tony, Trudy would too."

Jon smiled in spite of his subsurface anger toward his roommate. That Tony, he thought, what a hustler.

Tony showed up just then carrying his tray. Jon lowered his eyes and ignored Tony's presence, busily finishing his meal.

"Bitch," Tony snarled.

Jon knew right away he meant Martha Thorsgaard. Jon knew she had caught him. It's Friday the thirteenth, Jon thought. That could explain Tony's bad luck, in part. But Jon was too peeved at him to mention it.

"She remembered," Tony said. "She looked at me when I came back to nail down all those good courses and she said, 'Your name isn't Garpezi, it's Tarpezi.' She took my card, got a new one, signed it, then tore the other one in half. 'This time do it right,' she said."

Flyboy started to laugh so hard that he choked on his coffee and launched into a coughing spasm that made Jon jump.

"Got something stuck in his intake manifold," Shark said with a snicker from the next table, pointing at Flyboy.

Wide-eyed, Flyboy finally sucked in a deep breath but kept on giggling. "At least it half worked," he said, nodding towards Jon. "*He* got good courses."

Suddenly the whole toilet scheme seemed supremely absurd

to Jon. Carting it up to their room. Storing it for a whole semester. Toting it over to the gym. In spite of the ire he was feeling toward Tony, Jon couldn't help but smile. Talk about juvenile behavior, Jon thought.

Tony slowly began to smile, too. "You little sonnova bitch," he said to Jon. "It was *my* idea." He tapped his chest with his index finger. "I planned it all." Then he turned the finger accusingly at his roommate. "You got away with it, you little shit, and I didn't."

"Did you get a really bad schedule?" Flyboy asked.

"It's pretty lousy. Mostly I'm mad at that Bitchgaard for catching me. Next year I'm going to plan something absolutely foolproof."

"You need a new philosophy," Flyboy said. "Be stoic. Take what comes."

Tony just growled.

"I gotta go downtown," Flyboy said. "My car's in the shop."

Jon studied Flyboy as he walked away. A northern Iowa farm boy art teacher with chiseled features, Jon thought. In spite of all those adjectives, he might not be so bad for Trudy after all.

18

At seven o'clock in the morning on reading day, the Saturday before finals, Jon found a note in his PO box:

> Friday, 10 PM
>
> Dear Jon,
> I can't concentrate on studying for my finals. I'd like to talk. Could you meet me in front of the book check-out at the library? I don't know when you're free, so I'll be there tomorrow morning at 8:00—and again at 9:00—and again at 10:00—and. . .
> Holly

Jon wondered how much Holly remembered of their brandy Coke episode. He knew she had to be haunted by it. Almost a week had passed and they still hadn't talked about it.

Jon headed to the library after breakfast, and spotted Holly reading the bulletin board across the lobby from the book check-out.

"Hi," he said.

"Thanks for coming," she said, her eyes downcast.

"Let's go up to fifth stack and find a bench," Jon suggested. "We can talk there."

They climbed the stairs in silence, Holly in the lead. Jon studied her firm little body as he walked behind her. After only a week, he could no longer clearly visualize Holly with her shirt off. The improbable episode was already vague in his memory.

They found an empty bench on fifth stack and sat down.

"I'm so ashamed," Holly whispered. Jon could see she was close to tears. "I don't know everything I did at your parents' house, but I'm horribly ashamed."

"You didn't do much—except say some angry things about your dad's church. It doesn't matter."

"It matters to me. Drunk and half-naked? You must think the worst of me."

"No. I think you were like one of the furies—an angry daughter who loved her father very much."

"What all did I say?"

"You really want to know?"

"Yes."

"You called St. Olaf a damned Lutheran school. You called your dad's congregation a goddamned bunch of jackals. And you said you were tired of being a good, little virgin."

"Oh no," Holly muttered, shaking her hanging head.

"And then, you passed out. I picked you up and carried you in to my sister's bed to sleep it off."

Holly wiped her eyes.

"Look, Holly," Jon said. "I know you didn't mean any of it."

"Can you forgive me?"

"There's nothing to forgive. I've forgotten it already."

"Could we still be friends?" she asked, raising her chin a bit.

"Of course. You just go get ready to ace your finals. Is your first one on Monday?"

"Yes. And my last one is on Saturday. My parents are coming for me on Sunday afternoon. Then home to Forest Mills to help pack." She wiped her eyes again.

Jon hated seeing Holly so miserable. He grabbed her hand and squeezed it.

"Things work out," he said. It was the best he could do.

During exam week, Jon avoided Tony. His slurs at Rhonda were beyond enduring. Jon ate at odd times and spent several afternoons and evenings studying at home. His mother was pleased to be able to help out, providing him with sandwiches and cocoa and cookies as he studied.

Daydreams about Rhonda distracted Jon often during these cram sessions. He also couldn't help musing on what Tony seemed to be suggesting.

Jon finished his last exam on Friday at three o'clock, then went straight to his room. He kicked off his penny loafers, climbed into his bunk, and collapsed.

Jon dozed all afternoon, then went to bed early. He was only vaguely aware of Tony cramming most of the night. Although Jon awoke fairly early on Saturday, he pretended to be asleep until Tony had gone to write his last final.

While Jon lay in bed contemplating getting up, Flyboy opened the door, popped his head inside, and said hello.

"He's not here," Jon said.

"I know he's not. He told me he had an exam this morning. Actually, I came to see you."

"Me?"

"I need to borrow your car. The clutch is out on my Plymouth but I have to get home to Iowa to sign some legal papers. My dad's buying more land."

"Sure, you can take the roadster. But have you ever ridden in a convertible in the winter?"

"There's nothing warmer than a flight jacket," Flyboy said.

"Take a hat," Jon warned.

"Hey, why don't you come with me? You could help keep the windshield scraped. It'd just be a quick trip. We'll eat a couple of good meals and start back early Sunday—unless my folks talk us into going to church."

"Sure," Jon said. A trip south would be a good end to exam

week. It would be a chance to get to know Flyboy better, too. But best of all, Jon would be far away from Tony, escaping his maddening lectures about Rhonda.

Jon stuck a toothbrush in his pocket. I'll pick up my storm coat at home, he thought. He grabbed a scarf, his navy skullcap, earmuffs, and his chopper mitts.

Flyboy scribbled a note and left it for Tony. Jon glanced at it.

Hey Diesel Dork,

Jon and I are driving his car to Iowa. Be back tomorrow sometime.

Flyboy

They walked down the Hill to Jon's house and Flyboy asked about Trudy.

"She's home," Jon said. "I'll introduce you. She's been back from New York since my grandma's funeral."

Jon introduced Flyboy to his mother, then called upstairs to his sister. "Hey, Trude, come downstairs a minute," he said.

She came down barefoot and in her robe.

"You didn't tell me we had company," she said to Jon, frowning slightly at her brother. She fussed nervously with her hair and pulled her robe closed tightly at the neck. Jon had never seen her so flustered.

"Sit down, Trudy," Mrs. Adamson said, "and have coffee with Kelly."

"I'm going upstairs to get my storm coat," Jon said, "then out to check the car."

Jon spent more time than necessary pulling the ankle-length coat from the closet. He fussed with the fur collar then took a quick shuffle through his Rhonda artifact shoe box. He spent a few minutes weaving one long black hair through the comb's teeth.

Give Trudy and Flyboy a little time, he thought. An art teacher pilot Iowa farm boy for a brother-in-law. Maybe so. I wouldn't mind.

"Better keep an eye on those two," Jon warned his mother as he walked back through the kitchen. Trudy blushes as easily as Holly does, Jon thought as he shut the door behind him.

Flyboy offered to drive, so Jon dozed for the first fifty miles. The roadster was noisy and cold, and their breathing was visible and frosted the windshield as they sped south on Highway 65. For the next fifty miles Jon answered all of Flyboy's questions about Trudy.

Then Jon began to ask a few questions of his own.

"Tony says you were a fighter pilot."

"Yeah, I was."

"They've made you guys look pretty glamorous in the movies."

"Ha." Flyboy snorted. "That's because we had nothing to do between missions. On the ground they treated us like kings. We ate, slept, and banged around in the nearest town. We were bored, I think. But in the air it was never boring."

"Did you have it rough?" Jon asked, hoping Flyboy would keep on talking about the war.

"I bailed out twice," he said. "One plane was shot to pieces and the other just quit running. I crash landed three times. Tore the wings off once, flipped upside down once, and caught fire once."

He went on to describe landings with crucial parts of his plane damaged or shot away, and described, as if he himself barely believed it, how he had held up the damaged wing of one of his buddies' planes with his own wing tip.

"We landed like Siamese twins," he said.

Jon took a deep breath of cold air. "Boy," he said as he exhaled.

"I never got a scratch in the whole war," Flyboy went on, "and that was the worst part of it. I got more and more superstitious. My buddies started to call me C-L, Charmed Life. The longer that went on," he added with a deep sigh, "the more guilty I felt about surviving. I still do. So many of my buddies had such incredibly bad luck. They were barely hit, some of them—but they went down anyway."

"You can't blame yourself for that," Jon said quietly.

That seemed to be the end of the narration. For the rest of the trip they talked about the courses they had just finished and about farming.

The Paulsruds were a wholesome clan, Jon concluded immediately after he and Kelly arrived. At home in Iowa, he was Kelly—not Flyboy. When the Paulsruds learned that Jon's father was on the staff at St. Olaf College, they became even more gracious.

Kelly was the youngest child in the close Paulsrud family. Throughout that afternoon of visiting, whenever he showed irritation or frustration or let a slightly off-color word slip, it was clear his parents were worried about him. Tony was right, Jon thought. Flyboy had gone off to war innocent as hell. He hadn't come home the same and Jon could see concern especially in Kelly's mother's eyes.

Jon asked about the crops.

"Everyone planted wheat," Mr. Paulsrud said. "We had a bumper crop. Good thing, too. They're hungry over there," he added and pointed east. Jon knew he meant Europe.

Jon watched the milking and feeding in the barn. After a huge supper, Mr. Paulsrud stepped outside and stared at the sky. He came back inside with a shiver and a concerned look.

"Smells just like it did back in '41 when we had that huge blizzard."

"You think it's going to be bad?" Kelly asked.

"Smells like it to me. It's not my way to tell people what to do," he said quietly, "but if it was me, I'd head back to Minnesota right away." He slipped on a coat and went back outside.

Kelly looked at Jon, raised his eyebrows, and nodded northward. Jon nodded back.

"Smart idea, I suppose," Jon said.

"I just have to make one phone call," Kelly said, "then we'll go."
When Kelly came back into the living room, his mother handed him two paper sacks.

"A loaf of my homemade bread for each of you," she said, "and a jar of my county fair Concord grape and rhubarb jam."

Jon thanked her and pulled on his coat.

Mr. Paulsrud came in from outside. "I put a sack of chicken gravel in your rumble seat," he said, "for traction."

As soon as they turned onto Highway 65, it started to snow. The sky closed in and visibility with it. Jon drove and he clutched the steering wheel hard, his knuckles white, his eyes wide. His nose was only inches from the windshield, his breath coating the glass with frost. He struggled to see beyond the blinding reflection of the headlights on the wall of blowing snow. Flyboy kept reaching across the dashboard and scraping frost from the windshield.

"There isn't a single other car on the whole road," Jon said and laughed nervously.

"No one else is crazy enough," Flyboy said.

"Do you think we should pull over?"

"Why don't you let me drive," Flyboy suggested. "I've been through plenty of soup like this—and in an airplane."

They made it back to Northfield at midnight. The storm had diminished some by the time they drove into Jon's parents' garage.

"Are you going to stay here at your parents' tonight?" Flyboy asked. "I would if I were you. Those dorm bunks are like rocks. I can walk back alone, you know. I don't care."

"No, I'll sleep in the dorm," Jon said.

They walked side by side through the crunching snow without saying much until they reached Ytterboe.

"It's really late," Flyboy said as they started up the stairs. "Maybe you should sleep in my room. Not bother Tony."

"He hardly ever wakes up."

"I think you *should* sleep in my room. There's an empty bed.

Shark's already left for home. You could put on clean sheets."

Jon stared at Flyboy. Their conversation had taken a strange turn.

"No, really," Jon said. "I'll sleep in my own bed. Thanks for getting us back."

Flyboy shrugged his shoulders and sighed. "Maybe going back to your room *will* be the best thing for you in the long run," he said quietly.

Jon turned the knob on his room door. The door was locked. That's funny, he thought. Maybe Tony's gone overnight too. Jon set Mrs. Paulsrud's sack of bread and jam on the hall floor and dug his keys out of his pocket. He slipped the key in carefully in case Tony was sleeping. He pulled the bolt back as silently as he was able, then picked up the paper sack and eased the door open.

Jon was surprised to see a soft light cast across the room. In the dim light, he saw the lemon tree had been moved to his desk. The lemon was big now. It had grown to full size and had been bright yellow for more than a week. A single burning candle stood in front of the tree. Two wine goblets and an empty wine bottle reflected shards of candlelight over the walls and off the windows.

Jon turned toward the bed and squinted, trying to see through the dark room. Then he spied Tony on the lower bunk and suddenly Jon's eyes opened wide.

Tony wasn't alone. Kneeling astraddle him was a *girl*. Both were naked.

Her face was turned toward the wall. Jon squinted harder and then he saw her hair. Long black hair cascading down her back.

No other girl on this campus has hair like that, Jon thought frantically.

Without waiting to see more, he started to back away. Just then Tony opened his eyes and turned his head toward the door, almost as if he'd been expecting Jon.

Their eyes met for only a moment. Jon backed out the door, closed it silently, and ran.

19

Jon sprinted to Ytterboe's center stairway, then stopped. For the first time in his entire life, he had nowhere to go. Going home would have meant his mother and twenty questions. Going anywhere else meant going home to get his car.

Jon stood there, tears forming in his eyes, wondering where he would spend the night. Then he remembered Tony's homemade wire key to the attic. Jon turned and ran up the stairs, two at a time. There was enough light in the upper hallway to find the key on top of the doorframe and open the door. But Jon knew that he'd be in complete darkness and freezing cold as soon as he shut the attic door behind him.

Jon swung the attic door wide and let his eyes adjust to the dark. Barely able to see, he hurried over to the stack of mattresses. He pulled two off the pile and laid one on top of the other on the floor. Then he scooped an armload of brown army blankets out of the packing case and tossed them onto the mattresses.

He returned to the attic door and shut it, locking himself into impenetrable darkness. He groped his way back to the mattresses.

Unable to see what he was doing, Jon rolled up a blanket for a pillow then wrapped several other blankets around himself. He squeezed his enveloped body between the two mattresses.

He didn't sleep.

Images many months old and many times rebuilt swam in his mind—tender, beautifully framed pictures of Rhonda, his Land-O-Lakes princess, the two of them on a lake somewhere, in the woods, in a cabin, living the ideal life that popular songs elevate to the level of perfect ecstasy.

Why did they do it, Rhonda and Tony? Did they do it to me? Jon asked himself. Or just for each other?

The candlelight scene in room 223 played repeatedly in Jon's mind and brought tears to his eyes again and again. He knew he'd never be able to forget it—the candle, the tree, the wine, the two of them together. Tony was where Jon had dreamed of being for more than a year.

"Damn him," Jon spat into the darkness. "Damn him. Damn him."

Jon's curses didn't include her, though obviously she'd been a willing partner.

Curled up between the mattresses, Jon stared into a sea of overwhelming darkness.

At least he was warm.

For hours, he lay on his left side, staring at nothing. Gradually dawn arrived. He began to see a little cloud form each time he exhaled. He noticed that frost had collected on the wool blanket wrapped around his face.

He looked up at the stout rafters, barely visible in the dim light. He recalled the scene in *Giants in the Earth* when Per Hansa, distraught over the mental state of his wife Beret, stared at the barn rafter and the hay rope, contemplating suicide for a brief moment.

Jon had never before understood how someone might be hurt so badly, could feel so absolutely friendless and hopeless, that choosing death over life would seem the only way out.

But the night before, an ex-friend had dished him a platter full of understanding.

Jon knew he'd never return to room 223 Ytterboe Hall. He'd have Flyboy pack his things, then he'd head straight home for

Christmas vacation. Next semester he'd find a new dorm room—
or live at home.

Jon's bladder finally interrupted his thoughts. He crawled out
and stood up. Stiff from the cold and from lying on his side all
night, he hobbled around the attic hunting for a container. He
finally found an old pail.

Jon aimed the yellow stream into the makeshift toilet and he
studied his shriveled up phallus.

Why couldn't humans be like vegetables? he wondered angrily. Wouldn't it be better if people weren't able to do that with each
other—or to each other? Wouldn't it be better if sex weren't a part
of everyone's dreams and desires and plans? Why couldn't people
at least be like animals, copulating only to reproduce? This cold
morning, Jon hated the whole notion of sex.

He sighed and felt thirsty all of a sudden.

He stepped over to a window and tugged at the handle on the
lower sash, fully expecting the mammoth window to be painted
shut or nailed down. In spite of the snow piled high on the sill outside the window, it lifted surprisingly easily. The big iron coun-
terweights, uncovered in the unfinished attic, clinked and rattled
noisily on their ropes as the window rose.

Jon leaned out and looked at the campus below. Sunlight glis-
tened on the unbroken expanses of new snow. The sight was so
astonishingly beautiful that tears filled Jon's eyes once again. He
turned away, wondering how the world could be so lovely and so
sordid at the same time.

His thirst brought his eyes back to the windowsill. No one
would ever die of thirst during a Minnesota winter, he thought.
Minnesotans may freeze to death but they never have to die
thirsty.

He scooped a handful of snow from the windowsill and stared
at it a few seconds. Then he began to wash his hands and face, the
sudden cold sting sucking his breath away. Then he funneled the
snow into his mouth. It melted quickly and trickled down his
throat.

Feeling hungry also, Jon stepped back to the mattresses and sat down to his breakfast. He opened Mrs. Paulsrud's sack of bread and jam and unscrewed the tin lid on the green Mason jar, then pushed down the wax seal to get at the gooey jam underneath. I wish I had a coat of wax to protect me from contaminants in the world, Jon thought with a bitter snort and deeply furrowed brow.

He licked the jam off the disk's waxy underside then impulsively stepped over to the open window. He sailed the disk far out into the morning air. It sliced a small slot in the snow below. Come spring somebody's going to wonder why that circle of wax is lying on the campus lawn, thought Jon indifferently.

He sat back down, tore off a chunk of bread, then spread on gobs of jam with his finger. He licked the sweet residue off his fingertips then munched on the jam covered bread.

Suddenly Jon heard something. He sat up straight on the mattress, stopped chewing, and listened. There was a soft scratching at the attic door. Jon saw the doorknob wiggle.

"Jon?"

It was Tony.

Jon held his breath.

"I know you're in there, Jon. The key's gone. Open up."

"No, you sonnova bitch," Jon called through clenched teeth. "Go to hell."

"I've been there," Tony called back. "You know, I could kick the door in."

"And I could jump out the window."

"I figured you wouldn't want to talk to me," Tony said, "so I brought Holly along."

"How'd you sneak *her* in?" Jon shouted. "You've got a real talent for sneaking in girls, you bastard."

"Jon?" Holly said through the closed door.

"What do you want?"

"I want to come in so we can talk. Open up. Please."

Jon thought about that for several long moments.

"If he leaves, I'll let you in."

After some lengthy whispering beyond the attic door, Holly finally said, "Okay. He's gone. Now please open up."

Jon laid his chunk of bread on top of the loaf. Suddenly shivering, he wrapped an army blanket around his shoulders then shuffled to the door and unlocked it. Holly stepped inside, shut the door behind her, and stared at him. "It's cold in here. So what's this all about?" she finally asked.

"Didn't he tell you?"

"No."

"Then neither will I."

"If you won't tell me, how can I help?"

"How does a girl get into Ytterboe?"

"Tony told me to wear slacks and a parka with the hood up."

"You dressed like a guy," Jon said and scowled. "For someone who doesn't want to get kicked out of school, he tries awfully hard to make it happen."

"He did it for you," she said.

"I don't appreciate his favors."

"Do you want me to leave?" Holly asked.

Jon didn't answer that. He stared at their clouds of breath mingling between them. "He asked me to give you this," Holly said. She thrust a closed hand forward, then opened her fingers.

"I don't want that," Jon said. The lemon from Tony's tree lay in Holly's cupped palm.

"Well, it'll be the last fruit from *that* tree. Tony met me at the front door carrying the tub. He picked off the lemon and threw the tree out into the snowbank, tub and all. Here," she said, offering Jon the fruit.

"Hell with it," Jon said with a grunt. He grabbed it from Holly's open hand and hurled it at the ceiling.

A rafter nail high above their heads impaled the lemon. The yellow fruit remained suspended on the nail.

Holly walked below it and held out her hand. A few drops of lemon juice landed on her palm and she dipped a finger in the clear liquid and tasted. She made a sour face. Tears welled up in

Jon's eyes and he turned away from her.

He started to shiver again. Holly stepped over to his side, wound her arms around his waist, and squeezed him hard.

"Tell me what's wrong," she said.

"No."

"I can't help if you won't tell me."

"You are helping," he said.

He began to weep then in soft and anguished sobs.

Holly gently led Jon over to the open window. He stopped crying at last and they stood in silence for a long time, side by side, staring out the window. Holly's arms remained around his waist, her blond head against his shoulder, the blanket insulating him from both the attic's chill and the comfort of her warmth.

"It's beautiful this morning," she finally said.

"The snow down there is," he said, staring blankly out the window. "Other places it's pretty ugly."

"Tell me," she insisted again.

"No," he said. "Ask me in a hundred years."

"I won't be around in a hundred years. I'm here now," Holly replied. She began to shiver.

Jon opened the blanket so she could join him inside. They stood there for several minutes, the blanket around both of them.

"Have you had breakfast?" he finally asked.

"Not yet."

"I've got some good, homemade bread and jelly," he said. "Flyboy's mother made them." He stepped out of the blanket and tore off another piece of bread. Holly looked around, studying the attic. Her gaze settled on the impaled lemon high on the ceiling near the cupola trap door.

"Is that where you and Tony slept?" she asked and pointed at the trap door. "Up there?"

"Yes."

"Would you take me up there?"

"Why not," Jon said dispassionately. He repacked the breakfast in the sack and threw the blanket over his shoulder.

They climbed the ladder, Holly in the lead.

"Push the trap door up with your head," Jon said.

Holly raised it easily and lowered it to the cupola floor noiselessly.

They climbed into the cupola and stood there silently for a minute, shoulder to shoulder, looking over the campus.

"St. Olaf is a beautiful place," Holly said. "Even if I don't get to come back, I've liked it here."

"I always have too," Jon responded, frowning, "until today."

"Today isn't forever," Holly said. "Things work out, you know."

After a long pause, Jon said, "I'm glad you're here, Holly."

"So am I," she replied.

They wrapped the blanket around both of their shoulders, sat on the cold tin floor of Ytterboe's cupola, and ate their breakfast. They cleaned their hands afterwards with snow.

Sitting there wrapped in the olive drab blanket, Jon felt like army surplus, like a leftover from an important war—like something that had never been used, never called upon, never needed and of very little value.

"Now you've seen me at *my* worst," he said to Holly.

"That makes us even," she said softly. Then she added with a tiny smile, "At least you kept your shirt on."

That made Jon smile. The bitter December wind blowing across Ytterboe's rooftop had numbed Jon's cheekbones and the upturned corners of his mouth froze in place.

20

Professor Adamson closed the file folder and was reminded again of the obituary lying under it. He pulled out the obituary and read it again. Alpha and Omega, he thought, looking at the freshman year journal folder and the obituary.

"He's dead now," Dr. Adamson said aloud as he stood up. "I'm going to kick his ghost out of this building."

Adamson slid his middle desk drawer as far out as it would go. He saw the flashlight first and set it on the desk top, then rummaged through the junk in back until he found at last, in the far left corner, the tiny wire key that Tony had crafted fifty years earlier. He checked his key chain to be sure he had his own master key in case they had changed the lock.

He tested his flashlight, marveling that the batteries still worked, then slipped it into his back pocket.

He stepped into the hallway, shut his office door, and walked slowly up the stairs to the second floor.

He stood in front of the door. Room 223. He closed his eyes, inhaling slowly and deeply to steady his breath. Behind his closed eyelids he suddenly saw a candlelit panorama of passion, still vivid after fifty years. He unlocked the door with his master key, grabbed the knob, turned it, and swung the door wide open.

Dr. Adamson blinked. He blinked again.

It was a storage room now. Filing cabinets mostly. There was no desk, no chair, no double bunk bed, no lemon tree, not one pinup girl poster. It was much smaller than he remembered. He stepped into the room, leaned against the wall, and stared. He let himself slide down the wall onto the dusty floor, the flashlight in his back pocket poking his right buttock. He leaned to the left and grabbed it. He sat there, flashlight in hand, studying the old room. Many coats of paint applied over the decades concealed the innumerable nail holes that had held Tony's pinups on the ivory walls—always ivory.

Memories surged through Professor Adamson's mind.

He remembered three and a half uncomfortable years of avoiding Tony Tarpezi on campus. Jon had even dropped a course that they'd both registered for.

He remembered a year of wondering whether Rhonda ever found out that he had seen them making love. He wondered whether her half smiles that year meant anything, if they were because she knew or because she didn't know. He remembered wondering if by some strange, unwelcome witchcraft her beauty was waning. Was she gaining a little weight? Was she walking more flatfooted? Had she somehow at age nineteen passed her prime?

Professor Adamson remembered his sophomore and junior years when he dated a St. Olaf girl named Sonja, and then a Carleton girl named Elizabeth.

Holly's father took a job at the church headquarters in Minneapolis, so she returned to finish her degree without interruption.

Holly was an ever-present and always welcome companion. He talked to her about his current flames and she talked to him about hers. When both of them were unattached simultaneously, they spent even more time together—ate meals, went to games, went to chapel. They were devoted friends.

"Do you remember way back in the fall of our freshman year," Jon asked her after the Christmas concert during their junior year, "that night we drove to Cannon Falls?"

"Sure," she said.

"Do you remember how we agreed back then that it wouldn't be romantic?"

"I remember," she said, a knowing smile blossoming into her cheeks.

"Do you think it's time we tried it the other way?"

They agreed that it was and began with a lingering and long overdue kiss. Campus gossips had pegged them as a couple for years anyway. Some months they were aware that they had made far better friends than sweethearts. Some months they were both ready to give it up.

So many memories, Professor Adamson thought.

He sat there and gazed at the dingy walls in room 223 and at the rusty old filing cabinets. He tried to summon up the candlelit scene again—but the mirage had disappeared. The candle, the two wine goblets, and the lemon tree were gone. After fifty years he could no longer clearly visualize the scene. It's over, he thought. There are no ghosts here.

The only picture of Rhonda he could summon up at that moment was of the aging woman he occasionally chatted with at class reunions, the woman who had never quite made it as an actress, who had given up trying to make it in Twin Cities little theaters, and had married a hospital administrator. Whose first marriage hadn't worked. Who had tried it a couple more times and failed at those also, the last he heard.

Adamson pulled himself to his feet with difficulty, put the flashlight back in his pocket, and locked the door behind him. He returned to the center stairwell.

He slowly walked back downstairs to his office. He stared at his file cabinet for a moment, then walked over to it decisively. He pulled out the memoir drawer and reached to the back of it for the envelope marked RR. He opened it and pulled out the artifacts one by one—paper mementos, bakery receipts, an autographed community theater program, a note from their freshman year. After briefly studying each one, he dropped it in the recycling bin.

174

When all the paper was gone, he reached to the bottom of the envelope and pulled out a wad of chewing gum. He dropped it in the wastebasket and shook his head in disbelief at this fifty-year-old reminder of a youthfulness and supreme naivete that he could only barely remember. The last object was an old plastic comb. He suspended it over the wastebasket only long enough to notice the one long strand of black hair meticulously woven tooth by tooth back and forth through the comb. To the landfill, he thought as he let it go.

He walked into the hallway again and shut his office door. He returned to the central stairs and began to climb them. There's one more ghost haven in this doomed old building that needs exorcising, he thought. The attic.

In fifty years Adamson had never returned to the second floor, nor to the attic. But today he set his feet resolutely toward absolving all of these memories.

He stopped to rest on both the second and third floor landings, carefully locking all doors behind him.

The abandoned third floor looked like the setting for a drug war movie. The cluttered hallways were disturbingly derelict, a paradigm not only of his own advancing old age, but of how Ytterboe Hall now seemed to him.

At the attic door, he discovered the locks had been changed. He returned Tony's homemade key to his pocket and fished out his own master key. He swung the door open and stepped inside, locking the door behind him. The dim light of dusk cast eerie shadows through the dormer windows. He pulled the flashlight out of his pocket and clicked it on.

The attic hadn't changed at all in fifty years—the same huge windows with enormous cast iron sash weights, the same rafters, the same dirty pine floor, the same studs and joists and collar ties. Being in that attic was like being inside the building's rib cage looking for signs of osteoporosis.

After studying the whole structure, architects—or archeologists— would probably say that Ytterboe's attic was the only original space left in the whole building. A reincarnated Professor Ytterboe would feel comfortable only in the attic.

The ladder to the roof hadn't changed either. The only visible differences in the room were the absence of mattresses and the presence of a small mountain of broken furniture.

He studied the ladder for a minute, wondering if he could still climb it. Dr. Larson's warnings scrolled through his mind. Dying up there on the roof, though, Professor Adamson thought, might not be the worst place in the world.

He walked over to the ladder and began to climb slowly, steadily. He rested twice on the way up.

He pushed the trap door open with his head and let it fall open with a liberated bang, knowing it no longer mattered if anyone heard.

He climbed out of the hole puffing and stayed on his knees. His heart hammered like an air wrench. How wonderfully young I was fifty years ago, he thought with a sigh.

He rolled over and sat on his now substantial backside, remembering Flyboy calling his once skinny hind end a gluteus worthy of prime womanhood.

A warm spring breeze blew through his grey hair. The ubiquitous Northfield industrial aroma, toasting Malt-O-Meal, filled the air.

A few stars began to blink in the darkening sky above as he surveyed the springtime campus. The trees were lush again and a lawnmower hummed somewhere in the distance.

In one week the campus would be completely empty of students. In one week his office would be empty of all his belongings. In two months the building upon which he now stood so high in the air would be flattened.

But a wrecking ball couldn't touch memories. He stared across campus at the science center, trying to remember exactly where old Mohn Hall used to be. He looked down, recalling exactly where the Finseth Bandstand had once stood. They were gone now. Both of them. Ytterboe was next.

Ytterboe Hall had ushered him into the theater of his adulthood. This was the prologue of act four.

He looked toward the old gym, now the theater, and remembered the First Nighter. He looked north and remembered the accident on Highway 65, now I-35. He looked toward town and remembered a dimly lighted bakery and young melon-shaped breasts. Oh, how he had longed for her. He took two gasping breaths of fragrant spring air, then began to weep.

It's no one's fault, he finally told himself. This has not been a morality play. This has been my life. This is just how things work out. More of a mortality play, he mused.

He wiped his eyes and stood up. Nowhere else in town could a person stand so high and not be boxed in by walls and windows. High on Manitou Heights. On top of Ytterboe there were no railings and only twelve posts. In the cupola of Ytterboe Hall, he was on the earth's apex.

Dr. Adamson pulled a wrinkled grey handkerchief from his pocket and blew his nose. He cautiously stepped to the edge of the cupola and leaned against a pillar.

It moved.

"We're two of a kind," he said to the wooden post. "Not real solid on our foundations any more, are we?"

Then eighty feet above the renewing earth, standing atop Ytterboe Hall, Dr. Jonathan Adamson, Class of 1950, professor of history, shouted to the gathering darkness, "It's over, Tony. I'll try to forgive you now."

From down behind him, a deep, gruff voice replied, "I frickin' hope so."

Professor Adamson jumped. Heart pounding, he whirled around. How embarrassing to be caught talking to one's self.

"Oh," he said through a gasp, "it's you. You just about gave me a heart attack."

Holly's grey-blond hair gleamed in his flashlight beam, her head and shoulders sticking out of the trap door opening like a Jack-in-the-box.

"How come *you're* not puffing?" he asked. "I practically collapsed climbing that ladder."

"I'll tell you why," she said and chuckled. "Your mother weaned you on butter cookies and pork sausage, that's why."

"How did you get in? I locked all the doors behind me."

"Campus security," she said. "Rolf and I saw a flashlight beam waving around up here. I figured it was you, so he let me in. Are you okay? Can I tell Rolf we're all right?"

"I will," he replied. He helped Holly climb up through the trap door. Then he knelt and stuck his head down through the hole.

Rolf stood on the attic floor wearing a blue-grey uniform. With a businesslike air, he swung his great chain of keys as he looked up at the professor.

"I've told you your father was my scoutmaster, haven't I?" Dr. Adamson asked. Rolf smiled and nodded. "And that I had your grandfather for religion?"

"Yes, sir," he said. "You've told me that several times. Your wife insisted on climbing up there herself, sir, to check on you, otherwise I would have come up myself, sir."

"I'm fine, Rolf. And thanks for letting Mrs. Adamson in. Just leave us up here for awhile, okay? I have a key. I'll lock everything back up."

"I shouldn't."

"I gave you a B in history, remember?"

"Well, sir, please don't tell anyone I left you up there."

"Agreed."

Rolf said goodbye and quickly disappeared. Dr. Adamson stood back up. Holly stepped over and wrapped her arms tightly around him.

"I was worried," she whispered.

His shiver of response to her hug permeated his being as dramatically as it had decades earlier.

"I love you so much," he said.

She squeezed him tighter. "Not as much as I love you."

"That's what you think," he responded.

They stood there for a full ten minutes, linked together as friends, parents, grandparents, alumni—and lovers still.

"He set up an endowed chair in your name," she said, stepping back and looking him in the eye. "That's why they want you at the funeral."

"I suppose that means I *have* to forgive him," he said.

"Maybe there's nothing to forgive. He knew you were coming that night. Kelly phoned him from Iowa."

"How did you know that?"

"He told me."

"Well, the phone call didn't change anything," Jon said. "When Tony asked her up to the room he thought I'd be gone all night."

"But he had several hours to change his plans. He didn't have to let you walk in on them."

"You've known this all along."

"For fifty years," she said, wrapping her arms back around his wide waist. "He could have gotten kicked out of school, you know, for doing that."

"It wasn't the first time."

"Maybe it was. And besides, he did it for us, as it turns out."

"I guess so. I suppose," he conceded quietly.

"I'm just glad he brought me up here to you that morning," she said. "I think it was divinely preordained that you and I be together."

"Are you saying that Tony was an angel?" he asked.

"Rhonda once called him a dark cupid, remember."

Hearing Rhonda's name spoken aloud caused them both to fall silent—again.

At last Holly said, "Here, take this." She laid a hard, dessicated sphere in his hand. It was shriveled and black, the size of a plum.

"What's this?" he asked, shining the flashlight beam on it.

"It's a fifty-year-old lemon. I pulled it off a nail on the way up the ladder."

"I don't want it now any more than I did back then," he said. He turned and raised his arm as if to toss the wizened lemon over the hill toward the power plant.

"Don't you dare," she said, grabbing his arm. "There are seeds inside."

"They're dead."

"Seeds never die."

"I'm sure they'd be *very* dead by now."

"No, they are definitely not dead."

"Are you sure it's a lemon?" he asked, getting into the spirit of the old argument.

"Maybe it's an orange."

"No, looks more like a walnut."

Staring at Holly, Adamson was startled suddenly, seeing two images of himself reflected in her green eyes.

"He loved you," she finally said softly.

"I know," he said. "And it went both ways."

"Now," she said, taking the lemon from his hand and cupping it gingerly in her own, "let's go home and plant a tree."

THE FIRST FALL

THE FIRST FALL

STEVE SWANSON has taught writing at St. Olaf College for more than twenty years. His family history at St. Olaf, however, spans more than seventy-five years. His father, Cully, '25, Hall of Fame athlete, coach, Dean of Men, and Director of Admissions at St. Olaf, was resident head of Ytterboe Hall in the late 1920's and again in the middle 1940's. The author lived with his parents in Ytterboe Hall as a ninth grader in the forties, and as a college junior in the fifties. From 1946 through 1958, as a "townie" and perennial member of Building and Grounds Director John Berntsen's summer maintenance crew, Swanson worked in nearly every room in Ytterboe Hall. Years later, as a professor in the eighties and nineties, he had an office and taught classes in the building. Swanson is the author of twenty-six books, including middle grade, young adult, and adult fiction and non-fiction. He lives in Northfield, Minnesota, with his wife and is the father of five grown children.